The Mongolian Conspiracy

THE MONGOLIAN CONSPIRACY

Rafael Bernal

Translated by Katherine Silver

Introduction by Francisco Goldman

A NEW DIRECTIONS BOOK

Manufactured in the United States of America
New Directions Books are printed on acid-free paper.
First published as a New Directions Paperbook Original (NDP1270) in 2013.
ISBN 978-0-8112-2066-8
Design by Erik Rieselbach

Library of Congress Cataloging-in-Publication Data
Bernal, Rafael, 1915–1972.
[El complot mongol. English]
The Mongolian Conspiracy / Rafael Bernal ; translated by Katherine Silver ; introduction by Francisco Goldman.
pages cm
I. Silver, Katherine. II. Title.
PQ7297.B38C6 2013
863'.6—dc23   2013022656

10 9 8 7 6 5 4 3 2 1

New Directions Books are published for James Laughlin
by New Directions Publishing Corporation
80 Eighth Avenue, New York 10011

Contents

Introduction by Francisco Goldman   vii

THE MONGOLIAN CONSPIRACY   3

A note about the author by Cocol Bernal   215

Introduction

Filiberto García, the protagonist of *The Mongolian Conspiracy,* the sixty-year-old Mexico City police hitman, or *pistolero,* or *guarura,* as they are called nowadays, says "¡*Pinche!*" a lot, which Katherine Silvers translates as "Fucking!" *Pinche* past! *Pinche* furniture! *Pinche* gringo! *Pinche* Tame Tiger! *Pinche* professor! *Pinche* goddamned captain! *Pinche* jokes! Those are just the *pinches* found in the novel's first three pages. Mexican profanities, such as *chingar,* are famously variable, their meanings subject to context and tone and conjugation, and *pinche* can be used in lots of ways in Mexican Spanish, for example even relatively genteel parents might say, "*Pinche* brats, go to bed," but probably very few of their English-speaking American counterparts say, "Fucking brats, go to bed." But "fucking!" is certainly the best possible translation of the *pinches* in García's inner monologue, an explosive expression of rancor and mockery—including of himself—sarcasm, humiliation, bafflement, defiance, weary or bitter sorrow and resignation, all of which barely suggests the full range of his *pinches.* Let's just take a look at what the "fucking" "*pinches*" of those first three pages tell us about Filiberto García:

"Fucking past!" García has a sordid job and knows it, called upon by his police and politician superiors—who claim to be repulsed by killing and to belong to the modern world of legality and laws—whenever they want someone rubbed out. But García got his start as a killer as a youth in the Mexican Revolution, fighting with Pancho Villa and "the Centaurs of the North," when killing was manly and served a noble cause. "Here [in Mexico] all they teach us is how to kill," Filiberto García reflects later in the novel. "Or maybe not even that. They hire us because we already know how to kill." García was "born in the gutter," the son of an unknown father and La Charanda, perhaps a prostitute: and poverty and the instinct and struggle to survive, as with so many Mexicans, carved his course in life and made it seem almost predetermined. Better to kill than to be killed; killing was what he was good at, and so a hired killer is what he became. Filiberto García, terse and hard-boiled as he seems, is tormented by the past, the distant memory of the betrayed Revolution and the great generals he fought for, but most of all, he is haunted by all the people he's killed, usually men, but also women, and even a priest. His memories are like a cemetery in which all the corpses were put there by him, and those corpses take turns sitting up, as it were, intruding into his consciousness, forcing him to momentarily grapple with them before slamming the coffin lid shut again with a well placed ¡Pinche!

"Fucking furniture!" "He'd often thought about this furniture—his only belongings besides his car and the money he'd saved. He bought them when he moved out of the last of the many rooming houses he'd always lived in; they were the first ones they showed him at Sears, and he left everything exactly where they'd been set down by the deliveryman, who'd also hung up the curtains. Fucking furniture. But if have an apartment, you have to have furniture, and when you buy an apartment building, you have to live in it." Filiberto García has done pretty well for himself, paid to kill for the police and probably illicitly helping himself along the way to the cash that comes his way in the course of his "police work." He owns the building that he lives in. But his material pride is as sparsely furnished as his apartment. Only one other time in the novel is his landlord status even alluded to, many pages later, when, needing to remove the corpse of a man he's slain from his apartment, "All my tenants live quiet lives."

"Fucking gringo!" One of those intruding dead men from the past. In the mirror, Filiberto adjusts his red silk tie, the black Yardley-cologne scented handkerchief in his suit pocket. "The only thing he couldn't fix was the scar on his cheek, but the gringo who'd made it couldn't fix being dead, either. Fair is fair. Fucking gringo! Seems he knew how to handle a knife, but not lead."

"Fucking tame tiger!" "His dark face was inexpressive, his mouth almost always motionless, even when he spoke. Only his big, green, almond-shaped eyes had any life in them. When he was a kid, in Yurécuaro, they called him The Cat, and a woman in Tampico called him My Tame Tiger. Fucking tame tiger! His eyes might suggest nicknames, but the rest of his face, especially his slight sneer, didn't make people feel using any." Filiberto García doesn't stand for teasing anymore than he does for jokes. That woman in Tampico is certainly one of the very few, the reader will see, who could have been inspired to treat this hard predatory macho, who has always considered "bitches" as little more than "holes," with such teasing and ironical tenderness. "Out there in San Andrés Tuxtle, I killed a man then fucked his wife, right there in the same room, I raped her." But in this novel Filiberto García falls in love with Marta, a twenty-five-year-old half-Chinese woman, in a manner that will baffle, humiliate, transform and even redeem him. A good part of *The Mongolian Conspiracy's* almost sly and eccentric greatness resides in this love story, one of the most moving and unlikely in Mexican literature—and, without a doubt, the saddest.

"'Who would ever marry a man like me, Marta? With my ... profession?'

"'Many women. You don't know how good you are, the good you do in the world.'"

"Fucking professor! Fucking goddamned captain!"

"The doorman downstairs greeted him with a military salute:

"'Good evening, Captain.'

"That chump calls me Captain because I wear a trench coat, a Stetson, and ankle boots. If I carried a briefcase, he'd call me professor. Fucking professor! Fucking goddamned captain!"

His own air of respectability, the fawning it inspires, galls Filiberto, who has no delusions about what he does for a living. It's of a piece with the societal moral hypocrisy and corruption, the "lawyerocracy" of the modern Mexico that employs him, fueling his relentless rancor.

"Fucking jokes!" "Killing isn't a job that takes a lot of time, especially now that we're doing it legally, for the government, by the book. During the Revolution, things were different, but I was just a kid then, an orderly to General Marchena, one of so many second-rate generals. A lawyer in Saltillo said he was small-fry, but that lawyer is dead. I don't like jokes like that. I don't mind a smutty story, but as for jokes, you have to show respect, respect for Filiberto García, and respect for his generals. Fucking jokes!" "What's to laugh about in this goddamned fucking life?" "People who knew him knew he didn't like jokes. His women learned it fast." Only his friend, an alcoholic and impoverished criminal lawyer who spends his days cadging tequilas in cantinas, the only friend Filberto García has in the novel, dares to crack jokes at his expense. When the atom bomb was dropped on Japan, the lawyer turned and with a straight face asked García, "As a fellow professional, what do you think of President Truman?" Nobody else in the cantina laughs, only this drunken lawyer, who doesn't fear death but, according to García, doesn't necessarily have "balls" either, who in his dipso-maniacal ruination is a sole figure of integrity because he never expresses hypocritical reverence for "laws" and "legality" and he dares to rib this professional killer.

Pinche Rafael Bernal, he wrote so fucking well, especially in *The Mongolian Conspiracy*, and probably also in the other fifteen or so books he published in his life, mostly novels, some non-fiction, history, a volume of poetry, though almost all of those books are now out of print, all but this one, published in 1969, three years before the end of his life, and for years nearly impossible to find even in second-hand bookstores. Bernal, born in Mexico City in 1915, worked most of his professional life as a television and movie scriptwriter and as a diplomat in Mexico's foreign service. He is reputed to have been at least until the 1950s a right-wing Christian nationalist, even a Synarchist, and reputedly many of his novels were platforms for the didactic air-ing of his views, especially regarding his religious beliefs and the betrayal of the Mexican Revolution by the country's political, military, and oligarchic classes. He was also, in other novels, a *costumbrista*, a realist writer of local color and customs, obses-sively portraying the jungle as a corrupter of the human spirit and morality, and the ocean as its healthy and invigorating opposite. In a 1990 interview, his wife, Idalia Villarreal, who was fourteen years younger, described Bernal as a voracious reader of detective novels, by Agatha Christie and the like, and said that his first forays into the detective novel or *policier* before *The Mongolian Conspiracy* show the influence of Chesterton. She also described him as a serious reader of ancient and medieval history. The favorite books of his youngest daughter Cocol are Bernal's *Un muerto en la tumba* "where a geeky archaeologist turns detective after a fresh corpse is found in an ancient Monte Albán tomb" and *Su numbre era muerta:* "It is based on my father's experiences in the jungle and concerns a man who lives in a Lacandón village in the jungle of Quintana Roo and learns to communicate with mosquitos. I believe he wrote it when we were in Venezuela in the late 1950s." Yuri Herrera, the terrific young Mexican novelist, also admires *Su nombre era muerte*, which he describes as being about an alcoholic who retreats to the jungle, stops drinking, observes and studies mosquitoes and discovers their language, and then conceives of a plot to dominate the world with the help of the insects.

So how did Bernal produce *The Mongolian Complot*, this revered cult masterpiece that, though it didn't garner much attention when it was first published, has ever since so greatly influenced subsequent generations of Mexican writers? Writing it, Bernal seems to have thrown out everything that had previously characterized him as a writer, his approach to the novel itself and certainly the didactic expression of his convictions and beliefs—there is no trace of conscious Christian morality or devotion in Filiberto García, who, as we see at the novel's end, doesn't know a single prayer. Apparently nobody in Mexico had ever placed a character such as García, a *pistolero*, working for the police, one of the country's most notorious institutions, a denizen of Mexico City's lower-depths, at the center of a literary novel. (If anyone else did, nobody seems to remember that book.) In that character, Bernal created an unforgettable antihero hero. This seems all the more remarkable when one considers that Bernal, apparently a man of the right, published this book in 1969, a turbulent time when nearly every other literary person, writers and readers, in Mexico identified with the left, when the corruption of the political culture that had grown from the Mexican Revolution had been garishly exposed to the world, one year after the authoritarian governing PRI had massacred as many as 400 student protestors and others in Tlatelolco square in Mexico City, a seminal event which haunts Mexico and underlies its politics to this day, and in which many of the assassins who took part must have been order-following government gunmen of the Filberto García type, maintaining a stone-faced indifference to whether victims on the right or on the left. Bernal must have feared, or perversely expected, that García would repulse his contemporary Mexican readers, and that they would put the book down well before reaching the violent climax that, perhaps ambiguously, redeems him. For there comes a moment in *The Mongolian Conspiracy* when Filiberto García finally disobeys his superiors and fulfills his dark heroic journey with an act of sorrowful rage and vengeance through which he adds some final corpses to his memory cemetery—so maybe he hasn't changed that much, after all. But those killings are almost secondary to the narrative of his intimate transformation, which has another source, his relationship with Marta.

On the one hand this is a novel of suspense and detection, cleverly satiric, with a devastating political knockout punch, but even more memorably, it is a novel of the heart, and of a consciousness. The story is full of intrigue and violence, but the real action springs from its language. *The Mongolian Conspiracy* is narrated in the third person, while constantly, with beguiling agility, sliding into the verbal torrent of Filiberto García's inner monologue and commentary in a way that never impedes the taut unfolding of the story. It often feels like a first-person narration, until it suddenly reverts to a screen-filling image of García, as when, in Mexico City's little Chinatown speaking to Marta in the place of her employ, "García's eyes shone in the half-light of the shop," and we grasp the poignant vulnerability of that aging hard man's smitten gaze. The inner voice that Bernal created for his *pistolero* had rarely, if ever, been encountered in Mexican literature before, though anyone living in Mexico City who got around a bit would have heard it everywhere if she or he was paying attention, the voice of the urban barrio, of the cantinas, of harsh, violent deep Mexico, sardonic, fierce, profane, hilarious, pained, defiant, relentless, inventive, and aphoristic — "Fucking memories! They're like hangovers ... But the trick is to be like an old drunk and carry your Alka-Seltzer around inside you." It's a voice that reveals something essentially and enduringly Mexican, an embattled voice of daily and wily struggle against desperation and humiliation, and also one possessing a grandeur that isn't always delusionary; a voice filled with the bitter lessons of moral solitude imposed by life in the Mexican labyrinth of an extremely unjust society rife with mendacity, hypocrisy, corruption and danger at every turn, but also redolent of that unquenchable and paradoxical gift for "feeling" that one of the novel's Chinese characters tells Filiberto García, with biting irony, that his elderly and doomed compatriot, Mr. Liu, has absorbed from so many years of living among Mexicans. Nobody, not Carlos Fuentes, only Rafael Bernal, had ever brought that Mexican urban voice so vividly to life before, one that younger Mexican writers, in their various ways, have been mining ever since. When Bernal was writing this novel, he was serving as a diplomat for a sordid Mexican government in Peru. What an antidote Filbert García's voice must have been to the deracinated, often inevitably duplicitous language of the diplomatic report and the bureaucratese of an embassy. Speaking with my friend the Mexican novelist Martin Solares about the novel the other day, he speculated that perhaps in Lima Bernal had a Mexican chauffeur-*guarura* with a past in the police and who spoke like Filiberto García. Maybe, but I also suspect that as with an old drunk's Alka-Seltzer, Bernal carried that voice within him, and that he identified with his irascible gunman more than a little. His widow described him as "sarcastic, with an extraordinary sense of humor." Bernal was working as a diplomat in Switzerland when he died in 1972, three years after publishing *The Mongolian Conspiracy*, and was buried in Geneva. Borges, another supremely different master of the occasional detective narrative, died and was buried in Geneva too, rather than in his native Buenos Aires, and had his own nostalgic, complexly personal and even "literary" reasons for choosing that city as his resting place. According to Bernal's widow, he chose not to have his remains returned to Mexico, "Because he had the idea that it was horrible to transport a dead person from one far place to another. He told me, 'It's horrible to shovel the dead around like that.'" Add a "*¡Pinche* shoveling around!" and it would sound just like Filberto García.

While the pungent crunchiness of Filiberto García's language could not be more authentic, it would be a stretch to call *The Mongolian Conspiracy* a realistic novel of police investigations and international and political intrigue. The plot mixes Cold War "Dr. Strangelove" satiric goofiness with convincing Mexican Machiavellian political ruthlessness and duplicity in a manner that makes its riveting coherence seem almost accidentally *sui generis*. A Russian embassy source has reported to the Mexican government that there is a possible conspiracy underway, emanating from Communist China, to assassinate the President of the United States during his visit to Mexico. The life of the President of Mexico and "world peace" are also endangered. The rumor was first picked up in Outer Mongolia. The terrorists, who are not Chinese, have passed through Hong Kong on their way to Mexico, where they are supposed to make contact with a Chinese man. So have half a million dollars worth of fifty-dollar bills. The Cubans will play a role in the plot as well. It is exquisitely comical that Bernal centers this international conspiracy threatening world peace in Mexico City's very tiny Chinatown, on Dolores Street, a few restaurants that serve poor people's Chinese food to poor people, and a few shops, "one street lined with old houses and a scrawny alleyway trembling with mysteries." Filiberto García is a regular denizen of these cheap eateries, where the Chinese play their "forever silent and ghastly game of poker." Like these Chinese immigrants, he values keeping to oneself and keeping one's mouth shut. "There are things you don't talk about, or better, there's nothing you do talk about." Because his superiors know García is familiar with this marginal Chinese population, he is called into the investigation to find the Chinese man, and verify the conspiracy. That is ostensibly why he is given this crucial assignment in an international conspiracy. The real reason is because at least some of his superiors expect him to be a dupe, and for his "investigation" to leave a false trail of inevitable corpses. García is told that he will have to work with Graves, an American agent from the FBI, and with Laski, a Russian from the KGB. "You three will have to figure out how you're going to work together." This scenario, which might seem to offer broad farce of a Bullwinkle and Boris

Badenov sort, is actually handled by Bernal with great cleverness, insight and compelling, if essentially satiric, humanity. The mutually mistrustful FBI and the KGB men are "experts," highly trained and learned spies, fluent in languages, and politically knowledgeable. Naturally, they condescend to Filiberto García, if often jovially. "Seems like in the international crowd it's in fashion to be full of smiles. We'll have to see if they'd keep laughing with a bullet in their bellies." But the three men also know, for all their differences, that they are all in the very same business. "They know judo, karate, and how to strangle people with silk cords. The gringo uses a .38 special. The Russian a Luger." Laski tells the American, "One cannot govern without killing, Graves, my friend. All governments have learned this by now. That's why *we* exist." And Filberto García reflects, "I'm on Hitler and Stalin and Truman's team. Hey, you guys, how many dead have you got? But I'm very Mexican about it, which means I'm old fashioned. As you know, we're kind of underdeveloped. Just bullets for us." The most nefarious of García's superiors says, just before removing him from the case, precisely because he senses García is coming close to solving it, "Mr. García is not an expert in international intrigue. The truth is, he is not even an expert in police investigations." "Fucking international intrigue!" "Fucking Outer Mongolia!" After all, they are in Mexico City, which Filiberto García, not the FBI or the KGB man, knows how to read and decipher. García is the novel's detective, who methodically unravels the conspiracy, or rather its several parallel "conspiracies," though in one instance devastatingly too late.

Filberto García's heart is a greater mystery, to himself. Marta has fled to his apartment, and is staying there under his protection. Why? "Could it be that Marta wants me to kill someone?"

"Is Miss Fong an agent for one of the groups involved?" "Might be pure love, might be pure distrust." Even when she makes it obvious that she is romantically available, García treats her with chaste and considerate tenderness, like a "father. Fucking fathers!" His unacknowledged yet clearly inhibiting scruples about their age difference, and his own anxieties about the failing virility that comes with aging, torment him. "Fucking faggot!" he repeatedly taunts himself. "I didn't take advantage of her when she was afraid and now I'm not taking advantage of her when she's grateful." For the first time in his life, Filiberto García learns to feel unconditional love, and even how to merit it in return, and close to the novel's end, he actually seems on the verge of the most unexpected late happiness. "All I know is how to start down this road, how to live carrying my solitude. Fucking solitude!"

In this very dire, unprecedentedly violent and corrupt moment now in Mexico's history, Filiberto García's voice feels more urgent and more necessary than ever. Not silence but the voice within: it's the essential antidote, defiance, survival, the inexpungible road out of the past, where we can discover what we might be strong enough to finally give.

FRANCISCO GOLDMAN
MEXICO CITY, JULY 2013

The Mongolian Conspiracy

I

At six o'clock in the evening he got up from bed and put on his shoes and a tie. In the bathroom, he rinsed his face and combed his short, black hair. He didn't need to shave; he'd never had much of a beard, and one shave lasted three days. He splashed on a little Yardley cologne, returned to the bedroom, and took his .45 out of the drawer of the nightstand. He checked that the magazine was in place and that there was a cartridge in the chamber. He wiped it carefully with a chamois and slipped it into his shoulder holster. He picked up his switchblade, opened and closed it, then slid it into his pants' pocket. Then he put on his beige trench coat and Stetson hat. Fully dressed, he went back to the bathroom to look at himself in the mirror. The coat was new, and the tailor had done a good job; you could barely see the bulge of the gun under his arm and over his heart. Standing there looking at his reflection, he unconsciously lifted his hand and touched the gun through his coat. He felt naked without it. Once, at La Ópera cantina, the professor said that was because of his inferiority complex, but the professor, as usual, was drunk, and anyway—the professor can go to hell! That .45 was a part of him, part of Filiberto García, as much as his name and his past. Fucking past!

He went from the bedroom into the living room. His small apartment was immaculate, its Sears furniture almost brand new. Not brand-new time-wise — brand-new wear-wise, because so few people visited and nobody ever used them. It could have been anybody's room or a room in a cheap but decent hotel. There was not a single personal item: no pictures on the walls, no photographs, no books, not one armchair more worn out than another, no cigarette burns or rings on the coffee table in the middle of the room. He'd often thought about this furniture — his only belongings besides his car and the money he'd saved. He bought them when he moved out of the last of the many rooming houses he'd always lived in; they were the first ones they showed him at Sears, and he left everything exactly where they'd been set down by the deliveryman, who'd also hung up the curtains. Fucking furniture. But if you have an apartment, you have to have furniture, and when you buy an apartment building, you have to live in it. He stopped in front of the mirror on the console in the dining area and straightened his shiny red silk tie, then did the same with the black silk handkerchief in his chest pocket, the handkerchief that always smelled of Yardley. He examined his perfectly trimmed and polished nails. The only thing he couldn't fix was the scar on his cheek, but the gringo who'd made it couldn't fix being dead, either. Fair is fair. Fucking gringo! Seems he knew how to handle a knife, but not lead. His day had come in Juárez. Or, rather, his night. And let that be a lesson not to wake people up in the middle of the night, because the early bird doesn't always get the worm but the worms got that gringo.

His dark face was inexpressive, his mouth almost always motionless, even when he spoke. Only his big, green, almond-shaped eyes had any life in them. When he was a kid, in Yurécuaro, they called him The Cat, and a woman in Tampico called him My Tame Tiger. Fucking tame tiger! His eyes might suggest nicknames, but the rest of his face, especially his slight sneer, didn't make people feel like using any.

The doorman downstairs greeted him with a military salute: "Good evening, Captain."

That chump calls me Captain because I wear a trench coat, a Stetson, and ankle boots. If I carried a briefcase, he'd call me professor. Fucking professor! Fucking goddamned captain!

Night began to spread dirty grays over the streets of Luis Moya, and the traffic, as usual at that time of day, was unbearable. He decided to walk. The colonel had told him to be there at seven. He had time. He walked to Avenida Juárez, then turned left, toward El Caballito. He could go slow. He had time. His whole fucking life he'd had time. Killing isn't a job that takes a lot of time, especially now that we're doing it legally, for the government, by the book. During the Revolution, things were different, but I was just a kid then, an orderly to General Marchena, one of so many second-rate generals. A lawyer in Saltillo said he was small-fry, but that lawyer is dead. I don't like jokes like that. I don't mind a smutty story, but not jokes, you have to show respect, respect for Filiberto García, and respect for his generals. Fucking jokes!

People who knew him knew he didn't like jokes. His women learned fast. Only the professor, when he was drunk, dared to crack jokes around him. But that fucking professor, he doesn't give a rat's ass about dying. When they dropped the atom bomb on Japan, he turned to me with a straight face, and right there in front of everybody, he asked me, "As a fellow professional, what do you think of President Truman?" Almost nobody in the cantina laughed. When I'm there, nobody ever laughs, and when I

5

play dominoes, just about all you hear is the sound of the tiles on the marble tabletop. That's how men should play dominoes, that's how men should do everything. And that's why I like the Chinamen on Dolores Street. They play their poker and don't waste time talking or telling jokes. Pedro Li and Juan Po probably don't even know who I am. For them, I'm just most honorable Mr. García. Fucking Chinamen! Sometimes it seems like they don't have a clue, but then it turns out they know everything. There I am pretending to be a big shot, and all the time they're seeing what a chump I am, but they always, always, play it cool. Damn right I know all about their wheelings and dealings, their gambling and their opium. But I keep my mouth shut. If Chinamen want to smoke opium, let them smoke opium. And if kids want marijuana, it's none of my business. That's what I told the colonel when he sent me to Tijuana to find some guys who were moving marijuana across the border. Some were Mexicans and some were gringos and two of them ended up dead. But others keep moving marijuana across the border, and gringos keep smoking it, no matter what laws they've got. And the police on the other side make a big deal about respecting the law. All I can say is, the law is for suckers. Maybe all gringos are suckers. Because the law doesn't get you anywhere. Take the professor, he's a lawyer, and all he does is hang around the cantina mooching drinks. "If you get in trouble, he'll get you out." But I don't get in trouble. I did once, but I learned my lesson: if you want to go around killing people, you've got to have orders. Just that once I stepped out of line. I had good reason to kill her, but I didn't have orders. And I had to go all the way to the top and promise all kinds of things to get them to let me off. But I learned my lesson. That was during General Obregón's time, and I was twenty years old. Now I'm sixty and I've put away a small stash, not a lot, but enough to pay for my vices. Fucking experience.

And — fucking laws! Now everything's got to be done legally. Lawyers everywhere you look. And I don't matter anymore. Beat it, old man. What university did you go to? When did you graduate? No, sorry, you need a degree for that. Before, you just needed balls, and now you need a degree. And you need to be in good with the gang in charge, and to be full of a whole load of shit. Otherwise all your experience isn't worth a hill of beans. We are the ones building Mexico — to hell with you old timers. You can't do what we do. All you're good for is producing dead bodies, or rather stiffs — second-rate dead bodies. And in the meantime, Mexico keeps making progress. It's moving forward. The battle you fought is over. Bullets don't solve anything. The Revolution was fought with bullets — fucking Revolution. We are Mexico's future, and you're just holding us back. Move aside, out of sight, till we need you again. Till we need somebody else dead, because that's all you know how to do. Because we're the ones building Mexico, from our bars and our cocktail lounges, not your old-time cantinas. You can't come in here with your .45 and your trench coat and your Stetson. Much less with those rubber soles. That'll do in your cantina, for you boys who fought the old fight, you boys who won the Revolution and lost the old fight. Fucking Revolution! And then they come along with their smiles and their moustaches. "Are you an existentialist?" "Do you like figurative art?" "You're one of those people who like those Casa Galas calendar paintings." What the fuck is wrong with Casa Galas calendars? Well, it's just that Mexico can't be built like that: we'll call you when we need another stiff. Son-of-a-bitch kids got the jump on us. The colonel isn't even forty years old and he's high up already. A colonel and a lawyer. Fucking colonel! I'm better off with the Chinamen. They respect old people, and old people run things there. Fucking Chinamen and fucking old people!

The colonel wore English cashmere. He wore English shoes and tailored shirts. He attended international police conferences and read a lot of books in his field. He liked to implement new systems. People said he was such a tightwad he wouldn't even give you the time of day. His fingers were long and delicate, like an artist's.

"Come in, García."

"Yes, sir."

"Sit down, please."

The colonel lit a Chesterfield. He never offered one, and he sucked in as much smoke as his lungs could hold, not wanting to waste anything.

"I've got something for you. Could be nothing, but we have to take every precaution."

García said nothing. All in good time.

"I'm not sure it's in your line, García, but I don't have anybody else to give it to."

He took another greedy drag off his cigarette and blew the smoke out slowly, as if sorry to let it go.

"You know the Chinese on Dolores Street."

It wasn't a question. It was a statement. This fucking colonel and lawyer knows a lot, more than he lets on. He never wants to let go of anything, so he never forgets. Fucking colonel.

"You've worked with the FBI a few times before. They don't particularly like you, and they aren't going to like you working on this case. But they'll get over it. I don't want any friction— you've got to work together. That's an order. Understood?"

"Understood, Colonel."

"I don't want any scandals, either—no deaths that aren't strictly necessary. That's why I'm still not convinced you're the best man for this job."

"It's your call, Colonel."

The colonel stood up and walked over to the window. There was nothing to see but the building's dark courtyard.

Fucking colonel! I don't want any deaths, but you call me. That's exactly why they always call me, because they want people dead and want to keep their own hands clean. That kind of killing ended with the popular uprising, and now everything's done according to the law. But sometimes the law can only stretch so far, not quite far enough, and that's when they call me in. It was so easy before. Take out that bastard. That was it, no questions asked. But now we are highly evolved and very well educated. Now, we don't want any dead people or, at least, we don't want to give orders for them to be killed. We'll just drop a hint here and there, that way nobody's to blame. Because now we've all got a conscience. Fucking conscience! Now they're all squeaky clean, so they have to call in real men to do their dirty little jobs for them.

The colonel spoke from over by the window:

"There are only three men in Mexico who know anything about this. Two of them have read your file, García, and they don't think we should hire you. They say you're not a detective or a policeman, you're just a professional hit man. The third one supports you. The third one is me."

The colonel turned around, expecting to receive gratitude. Filiberto García didn't say a word. All in good time. The colonel kept talking:

"I've recommended you for this investigation because you know the Chinese, you play poker with them and you know about their opium dens. I assume this makes them trust you and will make things easier for you. In addition, as I said, you've collaborated with the FBI on previous occasions."

"Right."

"One of the two men against your appointment is coming here tonight to meet you. No reason for you to know his name. Let me warn you, he not only questions your ability to carry out an investigation, he also questions your loyalty to the government, and even to Mexico."

He paused, as if waiting for García to object. He wants me to give a speech, but speeches about loyalty and patriotism are for cantinas, not for when you're talking about a serious job. Fucking loyalty!

"Also, García, you'll be working with a Russian agent."

His green eyes widened imperceptibly.

"I know, that might sound like a strange combination, but the man you'll meet will explain it, if, that is, he deems it appropriate."

García took out a Delicado cigarette and lit it. There was no ashtray near him so he put the burned match back in the box. The colonel pushed the ashtray across the desk toward him.

"Thank you, Colonel."

"I think that you are loyal to your government and to Mexico, García. You fought in the Revolution with General Marchena and then, after that unfortunate incident with that woman, you joined the police in the state of San Luis Potosí. When General Cedillo led a revolt, you opposed him. You helped the federal government with those problems in Tabasco and with a few other things. You've done some good work cleaning up the border, and you did a fine job on that secret Cuban operations center."

Yeah, a fine job. I killed six poor slobs, the only six members of the great Communist operations center for the liberation of the Americas. They were going to liberate the Americas from their operations center in the jungle of Campeche. Six stupid kids playing at being heroes, with two machine guns and a few pistols. And they died and there was no international conflict and the gringos were happy because they could take pictures of the machine guns and one was Russian. And the colonel told me that those poor slobs were violating our national sovereignty. Fucking sovereignty! Maybe they were, but once they were dead they couldn't violate anything. They also said they'd violated the laws of asylum. Fuck the laws! And fuck the malaria I got in the jungle. And after all that, they come out in public saying I shouldn't have whacked them. But it was I kill them or they kill me, because they were very keen on being heroes. And in a case like that, I don't want to be the one who ends up dead.

The door opened and a well-dressed man entered: he was thin, with salt and pepper hair, and gold-framed eyeglasses. The colonel stepped forward to greet him.

"Am I on time?" the man asked.

"Exactly on time, sir."

"Good. I've never liked to keep people waiting or wait for others. Here in Mexico, we must learn to be punctual. Good evening . . ."

He held his hand out to García and smiled. García stood up. The colonel's politeness was contagious. The man's hand was hot and dry, like a bun right out of the oven.

"Have a seat, sir," the colonel said. "Please, make yourself comfortable."

The man sat down.

"Thank you, Colonel. I imagine Mr. García has already been briefed."

"I've explained that we have a special assignment for him, but that you and another person don't think he's the right man for the job."

"That is not precisely accurate, Colonel. I simply wanted to meet Mr. García before deciding. We have read your file, Mr. García, your history of service, and I am very impressed by a couple of items."

García remained quiet. The man's smile looked friendly.

"You are a man who is never afraid, García."

"Why, because I'm not afraid to kill?"

"As a rule, Mr. García, one is afraid to die, but maybe it's the same thing. Frankly, I have never personally experienced either aspect of the question."

The colonel intervened:

"García has previously worked with the FBI, and he knows the Chinese on Dolores Street. More to the point, he's never let me down, not on any of the assignments I've given him, and he's discreet."

The man, his friendly smile still playing on his lips, stared at García, as if he wasn't listening to the colonel's words, as if he and García had struck up a different conversation. He slowly raised his hand, and the colonel, who was about to say something, got quiet.

"Mr. García," the man said, no longer smiling, "based on your history, I think we can count on your complete discretion, and that is of capital importance. However, one thing is not clear from your file. There is no mention of your political affiliations or affinities. Do you sympathize with international Communism?"

"No."

"Do you harbor strong anti-American feelings?"

"I carry out orders."

"But you must have some philias or phobias, I mean, some sympathies or antipathies of a political nature."

"I carry out the orders I'm given."

The man sat thinking. He took out a silver cigarette case and offered it around.

"Thanks, I've got my own," García said.

He took out a Delicado. The colonel accepted a cigarette and lit it with a gold lighter. García used a match. The man smiled again, his eyes cold and hard:

"Maybe you *are* the right man for the job, Mr. García. I'll admit, it's extremely important. If we bungle this, there could be serious international repercussions and disagreeable consequences, to say the least, for Mexico. Not that I actually believe anything is going to happen. As usual in such a case, we have only rumors, suspicions. But we must act, we must find out the truth. And only the colonel and I can know what you discover, Mr. García. Nobody else. Understood?"

"That's an order," the colonel said.

García nodded. The man continued talking:

"I'm going to write down a telephone number. Call it if you have anything urgent to report. I'm the only one who answers that phone. If I don't, or if the situation requires it, call the colonel and let him know you want to talk to me. He'll put us in touch. Here's the number."

García took the card. It was blank except for a typewritten phone number. He looked at it for a few moments, then held it over the ashtray and lit a match to it. The man smiled, satisfied.

"The problem is as follows: as you probably know, in three days' time, the president of the United States will arrive in Mexico. He will be here in the capital for three days. If you want to see his schedule, you can get it from the colonel. It's already been made public. In any case, I don't think you'll need it. Protecting both presidents, the visiting president and our own, is the responsibility of the Mexican police and the United

States Secret Service. You'll have nothing to do with that; it is a routine assignment—for specialists, we could say. They are taking all the necessary precautions, and all individuals we believe might pose any danger have been identified and are under surveillance."

The man paused to stub out his cigarette. He seemed to be looking for the exact words to explain the situation and having a hard time finding them. The colonel looked at him impassively.

"A visit like this is always a heavy responsibility for the government hosting a foreign president. We mustn't forget, in addition, that if there is an attack, our president would also be in danger. And there's something else: world peace is at risk. This would not be the first war started by the assassination of a chief of state. Plus, we have the precedent of Dallas. You can see, Mr. García, why, even if it's only a rumor, we have to follow up on it ... We cannot take any risks. What we've heard is very serious."

He paused, as if to let his words sink in deeply. García sat without moving, his eyes half closed.

"I repeat, Mr. García, it is only a rumor. Which is why we must proceed with discretion. If there's nothing to it, all will be forgotten and that will be the end of it. The press will have found out nothing and we will not have offended a country with which we have, if not yet diplomatic relations, at least a budding commercial relationship. That's why discretion is absolutely essential. Is that understood?"

"Understood."

The man seemed to keep doubting his own words. He gave the impression that he didn't really want to reveal his secret. He lit another cigarette.

"First of all, we have to find out what, if anything, is true, and if there is some truth to it, we must act quickly to avoid a disaster. Or a scandal, which wouldn't do us any good, either.

That's one of the reasons I've agreed to give you the assignment. You do not seek publicity for what you do."

"It's not newsworthy."

"Right. This isn't, either. I see we understand each other."

"As I told you, sir, García is the right man for the job," the colonel said.

The man seemed not to have heard.

"Here's the situation. A highly placed official at the Soviet embassy came to us and told us a strange story. Just to let you know, the Russians do not usually tell us anything, strange or not. Which is why we listened carefully. According to the embassy, about three weeks ago, right around the time the president of the United States announced his visit to Mexico, the Soviet Secret Service learned that in Communist China, that is, in the People's Republic of China, there were plans afoot to assassinate him during his visit here. They told us they first picked up this rumor in Outer Mongolia. Then, about ten days ago, they heard it again in Hong Kong, and it was learned, apparently from reliable sources, that three terrorists working for China had passed through there on their way to America. You will notice I said *working for China*, not Chinese. According to the Russian police, one of them might be a North American defector and the other two are from Central Europe. We don't know what passports they're carrying. In Hong Kong, you can get whatever passports you want. Needless to say, we've already beefed up our border security, but we don't know if they've already entered Mexico or if they are going to show up with tourist visas and false passports. As I said, we have placed under surveillance any foreigners and any Mexicans who might pose a threat because of their criminal records or their ideologies. Many of them, during the visit, will take a short trip ... on us. But about three thousand tourists enter Mexico every single day. It would be utterly impossible to keep tabs on all of them, so our only option seems to be added protection for the two presidents, with armored vehicles and all the rest."

The expression on the man's face turned sad, as if it disgusted him to have to take such measures. He put out the cigarette that he had barely smoked and continued:

"This morning, the Russians gave us some more information. It seems the terrorists have been instructed to contact a Chinese man here in Mexico, an agent of the government of Mao Tse Tung. He will supply them with the weapons — it would be too dangerous to carry them over the border. Are you following me?"

"I'm following."

"Very well, Mr. García. We need to know if this Chinese man is here in Mexico and if this rumor about a conspiracy is true, and we have three days to find out."

"Understood."

"That is your assignment. You are going to spend time among the Chinese, you are going to listen for any word of recent arrivals or new activity among them."

"What if the rumor is true and I find the terrorists?"

"In that case, you will act as you see fit."

"I see."

"Above all, with discretion. If … if you must take violent action, do everything possible to conceal the source of the violence."

"Understood."

It seemed like the man had finished talking. He was about to stand up, then remembered something else:

"One more thing. With the Russians' permission, we informed the American embassy, and they insist that you work with an FBI agent."

"Okay."

"The Russians also want one of their agents, someone who knows a lot about the case, to work with you."

"You want me to cooperate with them?"

"Only in as much as discretion allows, Mr. García. Only if it is convenient. The American agent's name is Richard P. Graves. Tomorrow morning at ten sharp he will be at the cigarette counter at the entrance to Sanborns on Lafragua. At that precise time, he will ask to buy a pack of Lucky Strikes. You will greet him with a hug, as if you were old friends."

"Understood."

"The Russian is named Ivan M. Laski, and he will be at Café Paris on Cinco de Mayo at two o'clock, sitting at the back end of the bar, drinking a glass of milk. Understood?

"Understood."

"You three will have to figure out how you're going to work together. Don't forget to update me on the progress of your investigation. I repeat: we have only three days, and in that time, everything must be cleared up."

The man stood up. So did García.

"I understand, Mr. del Valle."

"You know my name?"

"I do."

"I told you, Colonel, it was silly to try to hide my identity from Mr. García. Now, all I can do is ask you to forget it."

García asked:

"Do the gringo and the Russian know who I am?"

"Of course."

Del Valle turned to leave. The colonel rushed ahead to open the door for him.

"Good night, Mr. del Valle."

"I would rather you continue to avoid mentioning my name, Colonel. Good night."

The man left with his friendly smile and his cold eyes. The colonel closed the door and turned to García:

"You shouldn't have told him you knew who he was."

García shrugged his shoulders.

"He wanted to hide his identity. He holds a position of great responsibility ..."

"So, he should have given his orders over the phone, or through you, Colonel."

"He wanted to meet you in person."

"We've now had the pleasure. Anything else?"

"Did you understand your instructions?"

"I did. Good night, Colonel. Just one thing ..."

"Yes?"

"Why so much cloak and dagger about meeting the gringo and the Russian? I could just go to their hotels, or wherever they are."

"Those are your orders."

"Good night, Colonel.

II

Mexico, somewhat coyly, calls Dolores Street Chinatown, a Chinatown made up of one street lined with old houses and a scrawny alleyway trembling with mysteries. There are a few shops that smell of Canton or Fukien, and a few restaurants. But there is none of the color, the lights and the flags, the lanterns and the ambiance you find in other Chinatowns, like in San Francisco or Manila. Rather than Chinatown, it looks like a run-down street where a few Chinese have dropped anchor, orphans of imperial dragons, thousand-year-old recipes, and mysteries.

Filiberto García stopped at the corner of Dolores and Artí-culo 123. In the fourth house, belonging to a Chinaman named Pedro Yuan, they'll be playing poker, a forever silent and ghastly game of poker. In the upstairs rooms, several old Chinamen will be smoking opium. Chen Fong manages that business, God only knew for whom, but it couldn't net much because the smokers are older and poorer by the day. For all I know he keeps them on for charity, like nuns who take in old people and cripples. Once, when I was sent after some opium traffickers in Sinaloa, I pocketed three tins and gave them to Fong. Ever since, we've been buddies. Fucking Chinamen! They've won enough off me playing poker to keep the whole lot of them dreaming. And anyway, why the hell do I want Chinese friends? So the colonel can give me assignments like this one and let me know that he's been keeping tabs on me, knows that I know them and cover up their opium dens. Fucking colonel! For all I know he knows about those tins, too. And then there's del Valle. He didn't want me to recognize him even though his mug shows up every other day in the newspaper. He must think a gunslinger doesn't read newspapers. I'd bet everybody and his brother in Mexico knows he's one of the many who have their hearts set on being president. Maybe they also wanted me to play the chump and act like I don't even know who our president is, or who the gringos' president is. Them and their fucking mysteries! Then they feed me that line about Outer Mongolia and Hong Kong and the Russians. For all I know, that Fong with his face of a chump is the agent of Mao Tse Tung. You never know with Chinamen. The professor says they're my real buddies and maybe that's true. They're alright. When I came down with malaria, they visited me and brought me fruit and Chinese medicine. And my own people, they never even knew, and they never stopped by. My buddies the Chinamen. Fucking buddies! Fucking Chinamen! And that half-Chinese gal, the one who works in Liu's shop, she's a pretty one, and sometimes she even leads me on. "Can I write you a letter, my lovely?" "Only if you write it in Chinese." For all I know she's Liu's daughter, but these Chinamen don't give a damn anyway. They're like the gringos. That gringo sheriff in Salinas, when there was that trouble with those wetbacks. He was looking right at me when I made a move on his woman and all he did was laugh and order another round of drinks. Fucking gringos!

An old Chinaman stopped in front of him:

"Good evening, Mr. García."

"Good evening, Santiago."

"You not come today?"

"Later."

"You look at shop of Mr. Liu, right?"

The Chinaman's laugh was weak, thick.

"Little Marta very pretty, very pretty."

"You got a dirty mind, Santiago."

Santiago walked away, laughing his head off. Fucking China-men. They're always laughing their heads off. And they walk like they're not even walking, like they're just floating on air. And they just go floating along from one place to another, from Outer Mongolia to Dolores Street.

He lit a cigarette and walked over to Liu's shop. Marta was closing up and Liu was hanging the wooden shutters over the shop windows.

"Come in, Mr. García, come in."

He entered the shop. Marta smiled at him shyly.

"Would you like a lychee, Mr. Filiberto?"

"Yesterday, you called me just plain Filiberto, my lovely."

"But that was disrespectful."

García's eyes shone in the half-light of the shop.

"Would you like to have dinner with me, Marta?"

"I can't."

"We can go right here, across the street. And you can tell me what I should order because I don't know anything about Chinese food."

"Mr. Liu eats there every night. He knows more about food than I do … Filiberto."

García smiled. His smile was cold, as if he wasn't used to smiling, as if he hadn't had enough practice.

"How old are you, Marta?"

"Twenty."

"Have you got a sweetheart?"

"No."

"You live alone?"

"In a room, upstairs. Mr. Liu lets me live there."

"You haven't got any family?"

"No."

Marta looked nervous, like she wanted to end the conversation.

"You don't want to have dinner with me?"

"I'm sorry."

"You don't want to be seen with an old man, that's it, isn't it?"

"You're not old, Filiberto. But it's very late, it's almost nine."

"We can go to the movies."

"Another time ... Filiberto."

"The way I see it, Marta, you must have a sweetheart."

"Oh, no, Mr. Filiberto. Who would even look at the likes of me?"

"I would, my lovely, 'cause when I see a beautiful woman—"

"Don't say things like that, you make me blush."

A man entered the shop and Marta went over to attend to him. The guy looks like a foreigner but not a gringo. He's too short for a gringo. He looks European, tending toward Polish. I saw him earlier, when I was standing outside, playing the chump there at the door to the cantina. Must be tailing me. They're already snooping around. Must be the guys from Outer Mongolia. Fucking Outer Mongolia! Crafty bastards. Hey, I got a buddy from Outer Mongolia. Your mother's from Outer Mongolia. I better get a fix on this shrimp before he starts showing up everywhere, like that lost soul from Sayula in the song, the soul who never finds peace. Fucking souls! Marta is hot, that's for sure, but I'll be damned if I'll ever get to do it with her. I've never done it with a Chinese gal. And she's just a kid. Maybe if I arrange things through one of the Chinamen, then I can do it with her. Like with that Carolina number, the one who was acting all highfalutin, over there on Doctor Vértiz Street. She wouldn't even let me borrow a smile. Till I arranged things with the owner of the shop and two days later she was mine. They even brought her to my house. All for two hundred pesos and a few favors I could wrangle out of the police. Fucking Carolina! I think it was part of their business plan—snaring chumps like me. For all I know Marta is a business plan for these Chinamen, and they'll let me take her home so I'll keep pretending not to know anything about the opium. She's worth at least two hundred pesos, and I've never done it with a Chinese gal. And that Pole, what's he talking to her about for so long?

At that very moment Marta handed the customer a package and took his money. Then she walked back behind the counter to where García was standing. Liu had finished with the shutters and was ready to close.

"Sorry about that, Mr. Filiberto."

"Is he a regular customer, Marta?"

"No. First time I've seen him."

García went over to the front door and looked out. The Pole was entering the restaurant across the street. García turned to Mr. Liu:

"Want to have dinner with me? Tonight I feel like eating chink food."

"Ah, Mr. García. Very honored, very honored to eat with so honorable man."

"Let's go. See you later, Marta."

The Pole was sitting in the restaurant, at a table next to the window. García and Liu sat down nearby. After staring at the menu that was in Chinese and Spanish, the Pole pointed to a plate. The waiter asked him:

"With mushrooms?"

"Huh? Oh, yeah. Mushrooms."

"You want bowl of soup, Mr. García?" Liu asked.

"You decide, Liu. You're the expert."

García's green eyes were glued on the Pole, who was gazing absentmindedly out the window.

"Many tourists around here, Liu?"

"No. This place only for Chinamen ... and some Mexican. Almost never see foreigner, almost never."

Silence. The good thing about these Chinamen is that you don't have to talk when you're with them. They seem perfectly happy when they're quiet. García and Liu ate bird's-nest soup and ribs with soy sauce. The Pole finished his dish, paid, and left.

"Seems he doesn't like Chinese food."

Liu laughed.

"I think honorable foreigner not used to poor Chinaman food."

"Have there been other foreigners around here in the last few days?"

"Why you ask?"

"Just curious. So many tourists visit Mexico ..."

"When tourists want eat Chinese food they go Casa Han on Avenida Juárez. Only poor people eat here ... only we—"

"It's perfectly good food."

"Very honored, poor Chinese food very honored."

García didn't respond. Fucking Chinamen! But that Marta sure is fine. And the Pole looks he's new to Dolores Street, like he doesn't know about anything Chinese. But those three from the Outer Mongolia rumor, they're coming from China and must know a thing or two. Fucking Outer Mongolia!

The restaurant had emptied out. García leaned over the table to speak to Liu in a low voice:

"You guys from Communist China or the other one?"

"I from Canton."

"Don't act dumb with me, Liu. Is your president Mao Tse Tung or the other guy?"

"General Chiang Kai-Shek."

García forced a little laugh.

"There's nobody can understand you Chinamen."

"Ah! Chinese language very difficult, very difficult. Many character, Mr. García ... Very difficult."

"Any of your compatriots around here belong to Mao Tse Tung's party?"

"Chinese very peaceful people, very peaceful. Very happy live in Mexico."

"What if Mao wins?"

"Chinese very happy here, very peaceful ..."

Fucking Chinamen! Can't ever get anything concrete out of them. Or out of that fucking colonel or out of that fucking Mr. Rosendo del Valle, neither. Marta must have been surprised when I said goodbye so abruptly. But maybe it's for the best. Got to play it tough with women, can't let them get too sure of themselves. Fucking Pole! Why the hell is he following me around? How would he know I'm investigating this crazy shit about Outer Mongolia? I already smell a rat, and I don't understand much about these international affairs. But they still went and hired me. I definitely smell a rat. Fucking colonel!

Liu sat deep in thought. Suddenly, he smiled:

"You go to house of honorable Mr. Yuan?"

"Just for a while. Gotta work tomorrow."

"Very dangerous for Mr. García play poker, very dangerous." Liu laughed guilelessly.

"The last few games have cost me a bundle, Liu."

"Game between friend, between friend."

"Yeah, between friends."

"I no go tonight ... many work ..."

García asked for the check, but Liu had already signaled the waiter that he would pay. García wanted to protest. Liu placed his hand on his arm.

"We Chinamen, we like you, Mr. García. You just like us— you no hear, no see, no talk. Three virtue every Chinese child learn ... three very good virtue."

They left the restaurant and crossed the street. Liu said good-bye at the door to his shop.

The game at Pedro Yuan's house was lackluster. Just him, Santiago, and Chen Po. García didn't want to buy any chips. The sweetish smell of opium wafted down from the room upstairs. García opened a window and called Yuan over. The others stayed at the table holding their useless cards in their hands.

"I need a little information, Yuan, my friend."

"Very honored."

"This is serious, Yuan. I think I've proved that I'm your friend and I never stick my nose into what's none of my business ..."

Yuan nodded. His face began to show signs of concern.

"There's a rumor making the rounds that I need to clear up before the police get involved and start finding out other things they've got no business knowing."

"Always bad rumor everywhere."

"That's why it's best if I'm the one looking into this, Yuan, to see if there's anything to this rumor."

"You our friend."

"There's word out about there being some Communist Chinese agents among you. Know anything about that?"

Yuan sat for a moment in silence. His small dark eyes were full of sadness. When he spoke, his voice was so low García had to lean over to hear.

"We exile in strange land. Our honorable father and grandfather buried in Canton, where they suffer much in their life. Always one warlord and then another warlord, very bad thing. And then the white devil ... And always hunger, Mr. García, always hunger. We all like animal, not like men who laugh and sing song. You no know about these terrible thing, very bad ... And always one general and then another general; one party and another party, but for us always same, always very terrible. And now you say about rumor that these terrible thing follow us here."

"Any Communist agents around here?"

"Nobody know what deep in heart of man, Mr. García."

"True."

Pedro Yuan was trying to control himself, but fear was spreading across his face.

"What you do if you find Communist agent among us? Agent of Mr. Mao?"

"Is there one?"

"I know nothing, Mr. García. I not political. What they do to us?"

The Chinaman's voice was trembling with fear. Fucking Chinaman! He's more scared than a rabbit in a foxhole. If he's their agent, those Communists are really up shit creek.

"They won't do anything to you, Yuan."

"You think?"

"But you have to tell me the truth. Mexico has welcomed you, and here you have found the peace you were looking for."

"Very true, very true."

"That's why you have to give a little, too. Mexico doesn't want any rebellions, or any trouble like that here. And I don't think you people do, either."

"No, we no want ... We want peace, Mr. García, much peace."

"So, have you got anything to tell me?"

At the table, Santiago was shuffling the cards absentmindedly. Chen Po was staring silently into space, but García was sure they were both paying close attention, trying to hear their words and watch their movements in case they revealed what they were talking about. Yuan moved closer to García:

"There's a restaurant on Donceles Street, a place called Café Canton," he said, almost in a whisper.

"And?"

"I know nothing, nothing for sure ... only rumor, always rumor ..."

"What rumors?"

"People arrived ... Chinese people, and from a different country ..."

"From Hong Kong?"

"No know, but some hear rumor and say much money there ... and before no money there."

"Thank you, Yuan."

"What they going to do to us?"

"Nothing."

"You want drink?"

"No, thank you. Good night to all of you."

There was deep, thousand-year-old anguish in the eyes of the Chinamen as they watched him leave. I should have told them not to worry, not to be afraid. They aren't going to sleep tonight. To hell with them—fucking Chinamen! And their "very terrible" things. What terrible things could they have seen that I haven't seen? What I'd like to see are Marta's legs. I should buy her a pretty dress. Broads always like that. Fucking broads! All that chasing after them for a little bit of a good time, and then they get boring as hell. Fucking Marta! Always wearing that same dress. I should take her to the Alameda Cinema and then to eat some tacos, just so we can get to know each other a little. But I've never done it with a Chinese gal. Maybe it would be better if I arranged things through Liu. They don't care. Plus, they're scared and they like money. And that fucking Pole. Maybe I should tail him, but I don't want to spook him. Better to make him think he's the one tailing me. That way, we'll be running into each other real soon. Fucking Pole!

A woman's voice called out to him from a darkened doorway.

"Filiberto, Mr. Filiberto ..."

García stopped in the shadows, away from the light of the street lamp. Instinctively, he placed his hand on the butt of his gun. Marta walked into the cone of light. She was wearing a small woolen shawl over her head. García walked toward her:

"Marta."

Not a single twitch of his face betrayed the least surprise, if he felt any. Marta walked up to him and began to cry. She made no sound, but under her shawl her shoulders were shaking with sobs. García placed his hand on her arm:

"Marta, what's the matter?"

"I wanted ... I wanted to talk to you. Please ... I have to talk to you ..."

"Whenever you want, Marta. I always want to talk to you, but you act like you never even notice me ..."

"Please, Filiberto, this is serious."

"We shouldn't talk here, Marta. People know you, and me, too. What do you say we go to ... to my ...?"

"Wherever you want, but please ..."

As she said this, she touched his hand that was on her arm. Her hand was freezing.

"Marta, you're cold. Let's go somewhere you can get something hot to drink. Come on, we'll take a cab ..."

They stopped a taxi on the corner. Marta got in first. García paused for a moment, as if he was having a problem with the door. About thirty feet ahead, a car that was parked sped off. Could be a coincidence, but that car sure looked like it was waiting for me. Fucking Pole!

"Donceles Street," he told the driver, "Café Canton."

Marta didn't say anything. She tried to wrap the shawl completely around herself, as if she wasn't wearing anything underneath. García took her hand very gently, so as not to scare her. She didn't pull it away.

"Calm down, Marta."

The girl had stopped crying, but her hand was cold and clammy.

"I have to talk to you ..."

"Soon, Marta."

García had sat down very close to the girl. He felt her young, firm body and her leg trembling against his. He should put his arm around her, but maybe not, not yet. With these gals, if you take it slow, everything works out fine. They're like wild mares, you've got to tame them little by little, with soft words and soothing caresses, always acting like you could take them or leave them. Fucking wild mares! And then there's that car. I think it's a Ford, it was following us with its lights low. But now

I don't see it. For all I know it was just a coincidence. Fucking coincidences! I smell a rat, and now I'm starting to see its tail. And this Marta, who's so fine, for all I know she's part of that stinking rat. There's already too many coincidences. For all I know she told them: "I'll get the old man where you want him, so you can give him a goodbye party. He's sweet on me, I can lead him wherever you want him." For all I know, all the way to Outer Mongolia. Fucking Outer Mongolia! That's what that bitch did to General Marchena. It's true he was asking for it, up to his elbows in shit. And me there at his beck and call: clean my shoes; brush my uniform; bring me a bitch; go the fuck to hell; and I brought him the bitch and the bitch put him right where they wanted him. Fucking bitch! For all I know they're doing the same to me. But Marta's much hotter than that bitch.

"This is it, sir."

"Come on, Marta."

Before going in, he checked the street. The Ford wasn't there. They went in and sat down at a booth.

"Have a cup of tea, Marta. It'll do you good."

"Thank you, Filiberto."

García had sat down across from the girl, facing the door, as always. I should've sat next to her. I'm turning into a chump, a real chump. Right here in this corner I should make a move, but pretend I'm just comforting her, of course.

It was eleven at night, and the place was still pretty full. He ordered a tea for her and a beer for himself. The waitress gave him a dirty look. A man appeared at the door and sat down at a table near the window and facing the street. He also looks like a foreigner, kind of like a gringo. Or by now I'm just imagining things. They must've slipped me something—I'm seeing foreigners crawling out of the woodwork!

"Cheers, Marta."

Marta smiled over the lip of her tea cup. She still had tears in her eyes. García pulled his black silk handkerchief out of his jacket pocket, leaned over the table, and dried her tears.

"You shouldn't be crying, not with such pretty eyes, my lovely."

"Thank you."

Marta took the handkerchief and finished wiping away her tears herself. Then she blew her nose, her little Chinese nose running like a leaky faucet. But now there are two guys at that table. I didn't see the second one come in. I think he didn't, I think he was already here. Fucking tears! But this way they'll think, when they make their move, that I haven't seen anything. They're definitely watching me. Is it because of Marta, or something else?

"Have some more tea, Marta. It'll do you good."

He held her hand that was on the table. She didn't pull it away. She has some mighty soft skin, just like the peaches back home. And those two guys are making a big effort not to look at me, but they aren't missing a thing.

"Mr. Filiberto ..."

"Just plain Filiberto, Marta."

"I know that you ... that you're with the police ... That's what they say at the shop ... No, please, don't say anything. They also say that you're not scared of anything and ... that you've killed many men."

"Is that what they say, Marta?"

"But I know you're a good man, Filiberto. If you've killed people, it's because ... because you had to, because you're with the police and some people are very bad ..."

"Why are you saying these things, Marta?"

García's eyes had turned hard. He pulled away his hand.

32

Could it be that Marta wants me to kill someone? Hey, I've done it for worse reasons.

"I know you're a good man," the girl repeated, "and that's why I know you aren't going to hurt me."

"Why would I hurt you, Marta?"

"Because ... because you're with the police and you probably already know ..."

"What do I know, Marta?"

"About me. That's why you've been coming to the shop and talking to me. I knew it wasn't because of me. A man like you isn't going to be interested in a girl like me, Filiberto."

Now she put her hand on top of his. Son of a bitch, things are getting complicated—what's up with this broad? Could she have something to do with this Outer Mongolia business? But then, they wouldn't have let her go out with me. No, she's got something else up her sleeve. And she's ripe for plucking, even starting to give me some wiggle room. Good thing I didn't go through Liu.

"When you started coming to the shop, I thought of leaving, running away, but I didn't have anyplace to go. Then you started talking to me and you said things that made me laugh, good things, and then I thought, you couldn't be bad like they say. Because I've known people who are bad, really bad, back there ..."

"Back there?"

"Yes, when I was very little. I lied to you, Filiberto, when I told you I was twenty. I'm twenty-five ..."

"You don't look it, Marta ..."

"I've always looked younger than I am. And then they killed my father. I almost don't remember him at all. The Japanese killed him in a bombing raid. And my two brothers went off with an army, in one of those wars they always have there. And my mother died of hunger and some nuns in Canton took me in. My mother was Peruvian, Mr. García. And there was a girl in the convent who died, her mother was Mexican, born in Mexico. Her father was Chinese and had brought her there with him and nobody knew who he was. And the poor thing died of the starvation she'd suffered."

"When did that happen, Marta?"

"About ten years ago. And then the nuns had to leave Canton and they went to Macao and they took me with them and they gave me the Mexican girl's passport ... that's the truth, Mr. Filiberto. I know it's wrong ... but it's the only bad thing I've ever done in my life and there were so many refugees in Macao and in Hong Kong ... and so much starvation and so much fear ..."

She started crying again and covered her face with the black silk handkerchief. Those two guys are still sitting there, like they're nailed to the spot. And Marta is in Mexico illegally. How about: if you don't come home with me, Marta, I'm going to have to arrest you? That would be one way to get things started.

Marta pulled the handkerchief away from her face:

"The nun who gave me the passport was Mexican and ... and that's how I've spent eight years in Mexico, in peace ... I don't think I've hurt anybody by it ... Only Mr. Liu knows the truth."

"And now you've told me, Marta."

"Yes, yes, I have. Because I know you're not a bad man. That's why I decided to tell you the truth ..."

"Drink your tea, Marta. Or maybe you want something to eat?"

"No, thank you."

"A roll or some toast ..."

"Well, okay, thanks."

García ordered the bread and another beer. The waitress kept giving him dirty, mocking looks. That bitch thinks I'm trying to pick Marta up, and she's right on the money. And those two guys still sitting there. To hell with them! I'm spending the night with Marta and tomorrow we'll see about that business in Outer Mongolia. Fucking Outer Mongolia!

"As far as I understand it, Canton is in Communist China, isn't it?"

"Yes, it is."

"You were born there?"

"No. In Liuchow. It's nearby."

"Also in Communist China?"

"Yes."

Then they were quiet while Marta ate her bread. I've got to be tough, give her one scare after another and before I know it I'll have her in bed and grateful to boot. And then I could take her to Immigration and do my duty by the law. Fucking law! If all Chinese gals are like this Marta, I say, bring 'em on. Those two are starting to get on my nerves.

"I don't think you killed all those people, Filiberto. You wouldn't be so good to me if you had."

"Do you know the owners of this place, Marta?"

"Mr. Wang? He buys a few Chinese things at Mr. Liu's shop, but they aren't friends. They don't get together socially."

"Which one is Wang?"

"The old man, sitting behind the register. What are you going to do with me, Filiberto?"

"What about those other Chinamen behind the counter?"

"I think they're his sons. What are you going to do with me?"

García turned to look at her. Marta's face was turned up toward his, and there was deep anguish in her eyes. Now's when I throw the law at her. Fucking law!

"I'm not with the immigration police, Marta. I've got nothing to do with them. I'm not with the narcotics police, either, and I don't mess with those fellows who smoke opium.

"So … you didn't suspect me?"

"No. Wait here just a moment, Marta."

He picked up the damp handkerchief and put it in his pants pocket. He stood up and walked over to the register:

"Got a phone?"

"Yeah, it's over there."

Mr. Wang was old, probably very old, but he looked nervous. He glanced quickly over at the two men who were sitting at the table next to the door.

"Got change for a ten?"

Mr. Wang silently gave him change. The restaurant had started emptying out and the waitresses were bringing him the checks and money. Mr. Wang made two mistakes in his calculations. García, not moving, stared hard at him—a smile on his lips and his eyes as hard as nails. Then he walked over to the telephone. One of the men at the table approached the register, as if to pay his bill. García started dialing the number when he saw Marta stand up and rush toward the door. "Fucking Marta!"

He ran after her and caught up with her at the door. Everyone in the restaurant turned to look at them. The two men had left.

"Where are you going, Marta?"

The waitress came over with the check in her hand. García gave her a twenty-peso bill.

"Keep the change."

He took Marta by the arm and they started walking down the street. Marta's head hung down:

"I thought you were calling the police."

"I am the police, and I don't like it when girls run off before we've finished."

"Please, forgive me, Mr. García, and, please, forget what I told you. Now I realize you can't break the law just to help me. But I don't want to go back there. I'd rather die than go back there."

They took a few steps in silence.

"What are you going to do with me? Are you going to arrest me?"

"Let's just keep walking, Marta. It's a pleasant night. Don't be afraid anymore."

Behind them, a black Pontiac started its engine and drove off slowly with its lights dimmed. These guys are definitely tailing me. They might be from Outer Mongolia all you want, but they're total jackasses. I've been on this job for less than three hours, and they've already got me in their sights. Marta could be in on it. All her tears and me here comforting her, like her dear old daddy. Or maybe they aren't such chumps and they want me to know they're tailing me. But—why? And why Marta's whole song and dance? All she had to do is say she wanted to be with me, she didn't need to make up a sob story. Fucking Chinese! Maybe I'll catch a bullet before I get to do it with Marta. And I've never done it with a Chinese gal.

"Do you have the passport, Marta?"

"Yes. Here."

She was carrying it in her handbag. An old Mexican passport. The Pontiac was still following them. Now they're going to shoot me in the back, no sweat, just happened to be passing by, and *boom*. He died because he was a chump. Had to happen one day, the pitcher that goes to the well once too often gets broken. But they probably don't want to take Marta out, too. Fucking Poles!

"Where are we going, Filiberto?"

"My place. We have to look at the passport and make a call."

Marta said nothing. She kept walking with her head bent. García took her by the arm. When he touched her, his hand trembled. Is it because I'm afraid of the Pontiac or because I've got the hots for her? I've never done it with a Chinese gal, and I've had my eye on for this one for a long time. But she should have acted offended when I said we were going to my place. Or maybe they told her to get me there. Just bring him where we can whack him easily. She is really fine. And those guys behind me. They're giving me the shivers up and down my spine. If they do me in now, I won't get to do it with Marta. And anyway, at times like this, I've never wanted to be the one who ends up dead.

At the corner of Allende, a one-way street where the traffic went in the opposite direction, he turned and pushed Marta against the wall. The Pontiac seemed to hesitate, then sped up and passed them. Only one man was in the car. García stopped a taxi and gave him his address. Marta got in without a word. The story this Chinese gal told might be true, but I'll have to take a good look at the passport, and at her, too. I've got a bottle of cognac at home. That always loosens them up. And come to think of it, these guys have no reason to be tailing me. Though maybe the Pole tipped them off—some international conspiracy. Now I've been promoted to the Department of International Intrigue. Holy shit! Next they'll tell me to go whack some jerk in Constantinople, where they dance with their belly buttons swirling around. The dance of the seven veils. How do they whack people in Constantinople? As far as I'm concerned, a dead body is a dead body in any country. Like bitches. They're all the same. But I've never done it with a Chinese gal, and I think tonight all that's going to change, with or without Outer Mongolia. Fucking Chinese gal!

He told the driver to stop a little before they reached his place. He got out, paid the amount on the meter, and looked up and down the street. It was empty.

"Come on, Marta."

Marta got out of the car. She looked up at the houses and the sky. García took her to the door of the building, opened it, and they went in. The entryway was dark.

"The bulb must've burnt out. This way, Marta."

He took her firmly by the arm. Truth is, I don't like this light being out. I also don't like what I saw from the street—one of my windows open, in the living room. Something's definitely up.

They climbed one flight of stairs. They stopped in front of his door. Apartment four. Dark in there, too. He put the key in the lock and turned it slowly. He drew his gun with his left hand. As soon as he felt the bolt slide, he pushed hard against the door and fell into the room. The club hit his left shoulder and he dropped his gun. He fell to the ground on his side. The man with the club came at him. Marta was standing in the doorway, not moving, and the man didn't see her. Or maybe they were in cahoots. The man raised his club and leaned over to hit him. García could just barely see him outlined against the dim light coming in through the window. As soon as he was within reach, García grabbed his leg and pulled. The man dropped his club and fell on top of him. Not bad, this guy, a contender, after all. The club rolled to the door and stopped. The man sat astride him and reached with open hands for his throat. He had already found it when García jammed his knife into his stomach. The man groaned but didn't let go of his throat. At that moment, Marta hit him on the head with the club she'd picked up off the floor. García stabbed him again with the knife, and the man rolled off him, landing face down on the rug. García stood up, took the club from Marta, closed the door, and turned on the light. It was the Pole. García leaned over and touched him. He was dead. Marta stood motionless, her eyes wide open.

"Is he ... is he dead?"

"Yes."

"I killed him ..."

García looked up at her. There was indescribable anguish in her eyes.

"I killed him ..."

García kept watching her. Her lips were trembling. She looked like she was about to vomit.

"I killed him ..."

"Do you know him? Look at him, look at his face, Marta."

"I can't ..."

"Look at his face!"

Marta took a few steps toward him and forced herself to look at the dead man.

"It's ... it's the man who was in the shop this evening ... When you were there and ... and you asked me who he was and if he came often ..."

García dropped the dead man's head.

"What's his name?"

"I don't know."

"You'd never seen him before?"

"No."

"You sure?"

"Yes ... and I killed him."

García stood up. Seems like she's telling the truth. Fucking Pole! He nearly broke my shoulder. And now Marta thinks she killed him with the club. This'll make things easy. I've got her now!

"I killed him ... It's horrible, but ... but he wanted to kill you, Filiberto."

40

García walked over to her.

"No, Marta. I killed him, with my knife. You'll see if you turn him over, it's still in him ... Anyway, thanks for the help."

Marta went over to the armchair and collapsed. The blood was starting to puddle onto the carpet. García didn't take his eyes off the girl. Her eyes were glistening.

"Thank you, Marta. I killed him because he attacked me."

"You're covered in blood, Filiberto."

"It's his."

He had a large blood stain on his jacket and down the front of his shirt. He sat down, next to Marta.

"You see, Marta, they weren't lying to you when they said I know how to kill. They weren't lying to you ..."

"He tried to kill you. He hit you with that club and then he tried to strangle you. I saw everything, Filiberto, and I can tell ... I can tell the police if you want. I saw it, he attacked you ..."

Marta's words came out quickly, almost sputtering, like sobs.

"That's exactly what happened, Marta. But look at us—first time you go out with me, and we already have a dead body ..."

He stood up and went into the bedroom and returned with a sheet. He covered the body. Marta sat in her armchair, not moving.

"Maybe you should go into the other room, Marta."

"It's not the first time I've seen a dead body."

Marta's voice was shaking. She's making a big effort not to vomit. That's always how it is the first few times. And once they start vomiting, there's no stopping it, like they were drunk. Better not give her any cognac.

Martha stood up. She left her shawl on the sofa.

"What are you going to do with him, Filiberto? I saw everything and I know it's not your fault. If you hadn't killed him, he'd have killed you ..."

"He's not the first person I've killed, Marta."

"What are you going to do?"

García went up to her. He had to step over the body to get to her. Marta looked up and straight into his eyes. García stretched out his hands and grabbed her shoulders. His hands were trembling. Marta moved toward him, without taking her eyes off his face.

"What are we going to do with him, Filiberto?"

He was slowly bringing his face up to hers. Marta kept staring into his eyes. *She is really* really *hot! And my hands are trembling like a schoolboy's.*

He kissed her gently on the cheek.

"Go into the other room, Marta. Or into the kitchen. Make yourself a cup of coffee. There's a bottle of cognac on the counter ..."

"You want some? I can bring it to you, Filiberto. You could probably use some ... Or if you want some coffee, I can make it ..."

"Yes, please."

Marta went into the kitchen. *I'm even more of a chump than I thought. Who'd have guessed she'd get so affectionate with a dead body in the room? And here I am, acting like a goddamned gentleman.*

He picked up the gun, put on the safety, and placed it in his holster. Then he uncovered the body and started to search through the pockets. A few bills, all Mexican. A pencil, with its point protector. Two keys on a nondescript keychain. The suit from El Palacio de Hierro, Made in Mexico. The shirt, too. *Gotta see his shoes, but it's not easy taking shoes off a dead body, they grip onto them with their toes. Fucking stiffs!* Pachuca Shoes. Common. *Seems this Pole is Mexican after all. And the people* who sent him—stupid sons of bitches. Or maybe they thought I'd be the one to end up dead. But if he'd wanted to kill me, he'd have brought a gun, and he didn't even have a fucking knife. Looks like he's from the North, a poor slob. Maybe he was just a thief, but that's one coincidence too many.

"Are you going to undress him?"

Marta was standing at the kitchen door, a jar of Nescafé in her hand. García quickly covered the body with the sheet.

"There's only Nescafé, Filiberto."

"That's fine, Marta. I just wanted to know who he was and what he was doing here."

"You take sugar?"

"Yes, please, Marta."

Marta went back into the kitchen. García walked over to the telephone and dialed a number. It was answered almost instantaneously.

"García here, Mr. del Valle."

"I'd rather you didn't use my name."

"As you wish."

"Something important?"

"I started investigating, and I think there's something to that rumor."

"What happened?"

"I was just getting started, very discreetly, and a man started tailing me, then he attacked me …"

"Did he try to kill you?"

"Don't think so."

"So … I don't understand why he attacked you."

"Neither do I. But it's strange and I wanted to let you know."

"You did well. This does seem to indicate that the rumor is true. Don't you think?"

"Maybe."

"What do you mean, maybe? The fact that you were attacked confirms it. Are you hurt?"

"No."

"Have you started investigating the Chinese?"

"Yes."

"Was your attacker Chinese?"

"No. Seems like he was one of us."

"Okay. Keep me informed, García. I guess tomorrow you'll meet the people we discussed."

"Yes."

"Good night."

They both hung up at the same time. Fucking Rosendo del Valle! And all his goddamned secrecy. And now I've got to get rid of this stiff. Fucking stiff! The one in Juárez was a proper corpse. This one is just a fucking stiff. And I've got to get that knife out of his ribs. Can't go losing a knife on every stiff. Better not let Marta see this. Sometimes the dead hold onto their knives. They get greedy. And I've taken a shine to that knife. Knows its trade all on its own by now.

He leaned over the corpse, turned it face up, and pulled:

"You want me to wash the knife, Filiberto?"

Marta was coming toward him with a cup of coffee in one hand and the bottle of cognac in the other.

"You saw what I was doing, Marta?"

"It had to be done."

"Yes, it did."

"I looked out the kitchen window, Filiberto, and that car that was following us, it's parked in front. There's a man inside, smoking."

"The same one?"

"I think so."

García took the coffee and sat down on the sofa. He put the cup down on the coffee table.

"A little cognac?"

"You aren't having any, Marta?"

"My cup's in the kitchen."

"Bring it here, Marta, and pour yourself a little cognac, it'll do you good."

Marta went into the kitchen and returned with her cup. García poured her a little cognac. She's going to sit down on the sofa next to me and then ... but that stiff is in the goddamned way.

Marta sat down in one of the armchairs. She looked up at García.

"What are we going to do?"

"You, nothing, Marta. You're going to go into the other room."

Marta took a sip of her coffee. She's fine alright, but she sat down pretty far away from me. Maybe if I tell her to come sit next to me she will. Then I put my arm around her, like I'm comforting her, with no bad intentions. Just like a father. Fucking fathers!

"What are you thinking about, Filiberto?"

"Nothing."

"You killed him in self-defense. There's nothing the matter with that."

"No, nothing the matter."

"You are so brave, and now I know I wasn't wrong. You are a good man and that's why they like you ..."

"Who, Marta?"

"Everybody ... Santiago, Mr. Yuan, everybody ..."

"And you, Marta?"

"I'm not afraid anymore."

They drank their coffee with cognac. Filiberto García delicately raised his pinky as he lifted the cup. Like a goddamned faggot. Pretending I've come courting, but with a stiff in the middle of the living room. More like a wake. But I never go to the wakes of my dead, of my faithful departed. Because the departed are always faithful to the one who sent them on their way. They always stick real close to me, and I'm always checking to make sure they're still really dead, that they're staying faithful to death. And here I sit, acting like an English lord.

"Don't worry about it, Filiberto."

"About what, Marta?"

"We both know it's wrong to kill, but you did it out of necessity. That man forced you to kill him. I know you've never killed a man except when you had to, for your work ..."

"Yes, Marta."

"I've seen a lot of killing, killings for no reason, because they could, without ever getting punished. Do you want another cognac? I'll pour you some more."

"Thank you, Marta."

"Do you want me to heat up a little more coffee for you?"

"No, Marta, no thank you."

"Your suit is covered in blood."

"It is."

"You should take it off and let me get the stains out."

"Later, Marta."

"We women are so foolish. I was afraid of you. I thought you were going to turn me in so they could deport me to Canton. Mr. Liu told me that if they found me, they would definitely deport me. That's why I never left his shop and he always hid me whenever you came ..."

"Yes, Marta, that's what fear does to us."

"No, you couldn't be bad. You said things that made me laugh and laughing is a good thing, isn't it?"

"Yes, Marta."

"You aren't married?"

"No."

"That's why you're always alone."

They sat in silence. Now is when I should make my move. Fucking stiff! It's in my way. But it doesn't seem to bother Marta. Like she's getting used to it. Or she's got something else up her sleeve. Any other gal would be crying, acting hysterical and going on about her honor and her virginity. Fucking virginity! With this one, it's me who's acting like a chump. But the truth is, things have gotten complicated. I'm not one to get spooked by my own shadow, but I'm not used to making love with a dead body in the room. Well, not usually. You've got to respect the dead. I make them dead and that's why I respect them. As far as I'm concerned, the night's already a lost cause. And things were going so well. Maybe all Chinese gals are like this one, spending the whole night talking. But then there wouldn't be so many Chinese. And then there's her idea about laughter being so good. That's one thing I don't understand. I've never thought very highly of laughter.

"Are you going to tell the police, Filiberto?"

"Don't you need to get home, Marta? It's almost two in the morning."

"I live alone. What are we going to do, Filiberto?"

García stood up and looked out the window. The black Pontiac was still parked out in front. It was the only car on the block. As long as that car was there, there was no way he could take Marta home. But Marta didn't ask what the dead man was looking for in my apartment. That's strange. Women are curious.

There's that rat again.

"Filiberto, I've been thinking ... I don't think he was just a robber. He was following you, from Mr. Liu's shop ..."

"He was in the restaurant, too."

"Why was he following you? And who's that man in the car outside?"

"I make a lot of enemies in my line of work, Marta."

"But you said you don't know him."

"No, I don't. Sometimes you have enemies you don't even know about. Go into the other room, Marta. There're some things I have to do."

"Are you going to call the police? I don't mind if they find me here and I can tell them ..."

"Go into the other room and turn on the light. After a few minutes, turn it off, but don't close the curtains, so they can see that it's off from the street. And don't look out the window."

Marta hesitated. García took her gently by the arm and led her into the bedroom. He turned on the light and saw that the curtains were half open.

"I'm going to go out for a few minutes. If anybody knocks on the door, don't open it and don't make a sound."

"Your clothes, they're stained."

"I'll be back soon. Turn off the light in five minutes."

He left the room, switched off the light in the living room, and by the dim glow coming through the window, he wrapped the body in the sheet and threw it over his shoulder. Good thing this dead guy wasn't a big eater. Fucking stiffs! You don't only have to make them, you've also got to carry them, as if they were children.

He went silently down the stairs and left the body next to the front door of the building. Nobody's going to be coming or going at this time of night. All my tenants live quiet lives, and even if somebody does come down, they'll just think it's a bag of laundry.

He went down a hallway near the staircase to the back of the building, through an inner courtyard. There, he opened another door and came out onto Revillagigedo Street. He walked slowly around the block and returned along Luis Moya. The car was still there. He's probably getting nervous, wondering what happened to his friend. It's strange, his friend being gone for so long, but he doesn't check on him, or take off. Maybe he thinks I haven't gotten home yet? But he must have seen the lights go on and off. Very strange.

He took off his hat, pulled out his .45, and put it in the hat. He looked like a peaceful citizen returning home late. The man in the car was smoking with his window open. García came up alongside him and stopped.

"Excuse me, can you tell me ..."

The man looked up and the .45 came down hard on his head. The man disappeared inside the car. García opened the door and pushed him to the other side of the seat. Then he opened the door to the apartment building, picked up the corpse, and threw it in the back seat. He put on his hat and put away his gun. The lights in his apartment were off. He got in the car, started it, and parked it three blocks away. Then he walked back slowly.

Together in life as in death, the way it should be. It would have been better to take the sheet, but it's got no markings, and there's no way for anyone to trace it to me. And even if they do think I killed them, that's why they hire me—to kill people. Fucking people! I figure these particular dead won't have many mourners and they're not going to stir up much of a scandal. But if they manage to knock off the president of the gringos

... Holy shit! What a difference between one dead body and another, between a proper corpse and a stiff. They keep me around to make stiffs when they need them. That's what I am—a stiff factory. And Rosendo del Valle's so honorable, so gullible. And the colonel's an ass-licker. He must think del Valle will be top honcho one day. At your service, Mr. President. Here's your stiff factory. And then there's this business with Marta. She must realize what a chump I am. And here I am with her false passport, and that's all I need to get her where I want her. They didn't even think to change the fingerprints. With that alone, Immigration could nail her. Fucking Marta!

He stopped under a streetlamp to look at the passport. Marta Fong García, born in 1946 in Sinaloa. For all I know she's a relative. But I don't have relatives in Sinaloa and anyway García just kind of stuck to me along the way. Passport issued in 1954, by the Mexican Embassy in Japan. This passport replaces number 52360, issued by the Ministry of Foreign Affairs on April 11, 1949. Everything neat and tidy, everything in order, except for the dead girl's fingerprints.

He opened the door to his apartment. The living room was dark. Marta opened the door to the bedroom.

"Filiberto?"

"It's me, Marta."

He turned on the light.

"Do you want another coffee or a drink?"

"A drink, please, Marta. Nobody stopped by?"

"No, nobody."

Marta came into the living room and poured him a drink. There was a dark stain on the carpet.

"Thank you, Marta. You aren't having one?"

"I looked out the window, very carefully ..."

"You shouldn't have."

"You aren't afraid of anything."

There was admiration in Marta's eyes. García finished his drink in one gulp and poured himself another.

"I don't have anywhere to go, so I read a lot, especially detective novels. I thought it was all lies."

García looked out the window. The street was deserted.

"I'm going to burn your passport, Marta."

"Burn it?"

"Yes. It could get you into trouble. We're going to ask for your birth certificate from Sinaloa. Marta Fong García's birth certificate. And that's who you'll be now forever."

He went back to the window. Marta was standing in the middle of the room, and she walked slowly over to him.

"You see, I wasn't wrong. You are very good, and very brave, Filiberto."

"Like the heroes in your detective novels?"

"You're just going to say that I'm a silly fool."

"I'm going to take you home, Marta. It's almost three in the morning."

"I can't. I'd have to wake up Mr. Liu to open the door for me and ... and I can't. If he knows I've been talking to you, he'll be furious."

"Why?"

"He told me not to talk to you. He doesn't want me to talk to anybody. He says it could be bad for him."

"Is he sweet on you, Marta?"

"I can stay here tonight, on the sofa in the living room, and tomorrow I'll go look for work. It's not difficult to find work and now that ... now that I'm not afraid, now that I know you're going to help me ... I don't have to go back to Mr. Liu."

García kept staring straight at her.

"Is he sweet on you, Marta?"

"You have to rest, Filiberto. Many things have happened and …"

"It's okay, Marta. You sleep in my bed. I have to leave very early tomorrow. I'll sleep on the sofa."

"But …"

"Go on, Marta, it's late."

Marta went up to him and kissed him gently on his cheek.

"Thank you."

She went into the bedroom and closed the door.

Now things have really gotten complicated. Fucking Chinese. So Chinaman Liu's got a good thing going. That dirty old man! He lifted his hand to his cheek, to where Marta had kissed him, right next to his scar. Now I'm really acting like a chump. A stupid ass. What kind of crap is this anyway? How did they find out I was in on this international intrigue? Maybe it's better this way with Marta. At my age it's better to take things slow, to enjoy them more, but I've never done that before. And what was that about only three men in Mexico knowing about this; and with me that makes four; and then the Russian; and the gringo; and those who gave orders to the Russian and the gringo. And the two guys in the Pontiac, but they don't know anything anymore. And the Chinamen at Café Canton. And the police in Outer Mongolia. And then, why did they put me on this investigation? Fucking investigation. We haven't even really started and already there are two dead bodies. Just stiffs so far, we haven't gotten to the proper corpses. And Marta is so serious, watching every last thing. As if she's used to it. And she chose tonight to go out with me. Couldn't she be trying to pull a fast one? And me, instead of taking advantage of it, I act like we're in some kind of daytime radio soap opera. Fucking Palmolive soap opera! With international intrigue to boot. As if there wasn't any competition. I'm on Hitler and Stalin and Truman's team. Hey, you guys, how many dead have you got? But I'm very Mexican about it, which means I'm old fashioned. As you know, we're a little underdeveloped. Just bullets for us. Sometimes I think it's only a question of quantity. The more dead you chalk up, the less you go out at night. The first two, they kind of bummed me out. The widow of that dead guy, Casimiro, she stuck with me for a long time. The dead guy, too. Some dead people become very sticky, like syrup. And there are times you want to keep washing your hands. And now that Marta kissed me, I don't want to even touch my face. Fucking Marta! As far as I'm concerned, she's playing a dirty trick on me. Like the kind I've played on others. So I'd recognize a dirty trick when I saw one, as if I'd cooked it up myself. I don't like so many people knowing my business. In matters like this, better to go solo. And even solo there are too many people involved. My left hand shouldn't know what my right hand is doing. And what good is it to blab about it. Blabber mouths don't live long. I keep my lips sealed, because fish die by the mouth. And me, I haven't been the dead one yet, not like my pal Zambrano, who got into trouble in San Luis Potosí. All because of his big mouth. Right there in Alfonsa's bordello, that's where they did him in. I wasn't there. I didn't kill him. But I let on that he was talking more than he should and then I stayed in my hotel room like a goddamned faggot. Would have been better if I'd gone and killed him myself. They say he suffered a lot, because they kept kicking him in the gut and didn't want to finish him off. Alfonsa, being his lover and all, she asked them to get it over with. But the guys who did it didn't know what they were doing.

Seems they got scared. They say one of them even wet himself. I should have done it myself. It was the least I could have done for my pal Zambrano. Make sure he had a good death, one any loyal soul deserves. Zambrano had a way with bitches. For better or for worse, not a single one ever left him. And there's Marta in the bedroom and me here like Vasconcelos with my memories. Fucking faggot! And the next night, at the wake, I did it with Alfonsa. She smelled like a woman in mourning. From that day on she had it in for me. For all I know she knew something. Fucking Alfonsa! She was hot. And now, what am I doing with all these memories? Nobody can live off memories, only people who haven't done anything. Fucking memories! They're like hangovers. That's why drunks vomit, so they don't have to re-member, and beginners vomit after their first hit, like they were trying to get rid of it. But the trick is to be like an old drunk and carry your Alka-Seltzer around inside you. That way it all stays put and everything that stays put turns into memories. Good thing not everything stays put. Especially from when you're a kid and really a chump. Sometimes I think I've finally forgotten that gal's name, Gabriela Cisneros. Why remember a woman's name? One woman is like any other. All with their little holes. Gabriela Cisneros. There I was, just a boy, and on my knees to her, and finally she let me have a go. And Romualdo Cisneros found us out in that orchard in Yurécuaro. She was almost naked already. And right then and there, Mr. Cisneros made me get down on my knees on the ground, for real, and lower my pants, and he started whipping me with his machete. Right there, right in front of Gabriela Cisneros. And I started crying and I told him I wanted to marry her and Mr. Cisneros kicked me in the mouth. And Gabriela Cisneros pretended like she was crying, but she was laughing. She didn't even cover up her legs. And there I was, crying, with my naked butt in the air, red, as if blushing with shame. And Mr. Cisneros said he didn't want the son of La Charanda for a son-in-law. That's what they called my old lady, same as the rum they drank back there. I never knew what they called my old man, because I never knew who he was. A few years later I went back to Yurécuaro. Must have been around '29 or '30, and Romualdo Cisneros had already left for the capital and Gabriela had run off with a lieutenant, who'd left her in Santa Lucrecia or somewhere around there, pregnant. Some things stay inside, especially things like that, things that are left half done. That's why I don't like to leave things half done. Not international intrigue and not this business with Marta. And you also learn not to talk too much. There are things you don't talk about. Or better, there's nothing you do talk about. So you don't end up like my pal Zambrano, whose big mouth got him killed. Only bitches go around blabbing everything, at least what they want to. And that's why it's best to do it with a bitch once or twice and then walk away. Fucking bitches! And so you don't start blabbing, you're better off forgetting. What if I tell Marta everything? Like about how my butt was red from the whipping, as if ashamed. Like about my pal Zambrano. Instead of telling her things I should be in bed with her. Fucking Marta! For all I know she's laughing at me. But maybe things will turn out better this way, by taking it nice and easy.

III

García here, Colonel."

"Aren't you at your meeting?"

"I'm in Sanborns, and I've got my eye on the cigarette counter."

"The person who was here yesterday, he called me earlier today."

"I talked to him last night. There's nothing new to report."

"You're not going to tell him about the two men the police found in a car, three blocks from your house? They were both dead."

"Oh, that."

"What do you know about it, García?"

"One of them tried to kill me, the one who was stabbed. Do they know who they were?"

"Listen, García, I brought you in on this investigation to find out what's really going on, not so you can liquidate anybody who runs afoul of you."

"I think they're in on it. Do they know who they are?"

"In on it! The one you stabbed was a Mexican citizen, though, granted, not an upstanding one, but Mexican, in any case. I thought you'd be investigating the Chinese."

"That's what I have been doing, Colonel. Do you have a name?"

"Luciano Manrique, a man of many trades. Specialist in armed robberies. Ring a bell, García?"

"I didn't know him. And the other?"

"Also Mexican. A gunslinger from the north, from Baja. Roque Villegas Vargas or at least that's the name he used."

"Not one of my acquaintances, either."

"Now they're both dead."

"So it seems."

"Whatever you say, I don't see what connection they could have had with our investigation. Unless you have something concrete?"

"No, Colonel, I don't. What puzzles me is, you'd just given me this assignment, and I'd only just started talking to the Chinese, and then those two show up and try to knock me out of the game. Maybe the Outer Mongolians plan to hire local talent instead of using imports."

"Who knows. Maybe they had it in for you for something else. A lot of people have it in for you, García."

"That's true, Colonel, but I'm not too keen on coincidences like this."

"If you'd had a chance to ask them ..."

"Excuse me, Colonel, the gringo's here. I'll keep you posted."

He hung up and turned toward the entrance to Sanborns. A man had approached the cigarette counter and was waiting for the attendant. It was ten sharp. García started walking toward him. This gringo knows his trade. He's not looking around, not even out of the corner of his eye. Like he's only buying cigarettes. But I don't like that he already saw me. Fucking gringo!

The attendant went up to the gringo, a big smile on her face.

"Lucky Strikes, please, Miss."

García slapped him on the back.

"Hey ... what you doing here, old pal?"

"My friend García."

They exchanged a big hug, patting each other heartily on the back. These fucking gringos, ever since they found out we hug each other, damn if they don't overdo it.

"I think I'm being followed," García said.

The gringo didn't decrease the width of his smile. The young lady behind the counter spoke to him curtly:

"Your cigarettes, sir."

Graves extricated himself from the embrace, picked up the cigarettes, and paid. Then he turned to García. He was smiling like a man who'd just run into a very good friend he hadn't seen in a long time—all enthusiasm and joy. The smile didn't change one iota when he said, "I know. Me, too."

"What a pleasure to see you," García said.

The American was about forty years old, short and strong. This gringo's got the muscles of a boxer and the face of a son-ofabitch. Not a bad combination in a man who knows his trade, and it looks like this one does. And with those little gold-rimmed eyeglasses, that fedora, and his colorful belt, he looks like a travel agent. Fucking gringos! They're always playing some part. Me, even if I wear that little hat and those glasses, I'd still look like what I am: a stiff factory. Even the cigarette broad was horrified that he was friends with me. She must think he's a tourist and doesn't understand these *latinos*, that he's got no idea who he's dealing with. Fucking broad! And she isn't even much to look at.

The gringo had taken him by the arm and was leading him into the restaurant.

"You've already eaten breakfast, García, my friend? Come on, at least have a cup of coffee with me."

"Love to."

Few people were eating breakfast at that hour, so they found a table set a little apart and sat down. They were keeping a close eye on each other, the American with his tourist grin not losing his idiotic bliss for a single second. You can tell just by looking at his hands that this gringo does karate. He must know more tricks than an old fox. And with that little smile, I'll bet he's one of those guys who kills without even blinking. Has Marta woken up? Has she read my note? For all I know, she's already gone, her little mission accomplished. She did as she was told and got me where they wanted me. Can't say the same for the other two. That's why they're dead.

Graves's breakfast came—eggs and ham, toast and orange juice. García had a coffee. Fucking coffee! Tastes like dirty water, but that's the way gringos like it. And then, they use cream instead of milk; you'd think they were eating *chilaquiles*.

The American talked between bites, always smiling and pleasant:

"We've already done some preliminary investigations, Mr. García, starting with you."

"And ..."

"No offense. It's par for the course in our organization."

"What else have you been investigating?"

"First off, all travelers arriving in Mexico from Asia, either through the United States or through Canada. We've already located most of them and eliminated them from the list. In fact, there are only five we haven't yet located and four of them are suspicious. Two of them arrived together, by Canadian Pacific, directly from Hong Kong, and we've lost track of them here in

Mexico. But their particulars don't match those we got from our Russian colleagues. One is Chinese, but a Cuban citizen. The other is from the States, an adventurer who was in China and Indonesia, and was a pilot in the Korean War. One of our pilots, Mr. García."

"Looks like he outgrew his crate."

Graves stared at him, his smile fading from his lips.

"I don't understand."

"It's just an expression we use. What I mean is maybe that pilot isn't so keen on helping you fight Communism anymore."

"Oh, now I get it. Exactly. We think he's defected. But he still has his American passport, which makes it easy for him to travel, as long as he doesn't enter the U.S. The Chinese man is using a Mexican passport, false, according to the authorities. Apparently in Asia he was using a Cuban passport. As you can see, we've made some headway in our investigations."

"Yes."

"But it's not enough. Others could have come here via other routes. They could have come through the United States and changed passports there. It's almost impossible, in such a short time, to have a fix on everybody who's traveled from Asia to America. They also could have come through Europe. That's why we reached the conclusion that the real investigation has to be carried out here in Mexico."

"Really, you don't say."

"The American we haven't located goes by the name of James P. Moran and the Chinaman is Xavier Liu. Maybe, given your contacts in the Chinese community, we'll be able to find them."

"Maybe."

"We understand you were given your orders last night, and you're only now getting started. Right?"

"Right."

There was silence. *This goddamned gringo already wants to start giving me orders. I don't think I have to tell him everything. What he doesn't know won't hurt him. And if I tell him about Marta, he's going to want to investigate her, too. Fucking gringo. That's right: the less said, the better.*

"We are supposed to meet our Russian colleague," Graves said. "Those are the orders."

"Right."

"We're supposed to cooperate with him on everything, but I don't think that means we have to share everything. Don't you agree, Mr. García? We can't trust him completely, not after everything that's happened."

"In this profession, you can't trust anything or anybody."

Graves flashed his full tourist smile.

"Well, there are some things you *can* trust. Like the FBI."

"You think?"

"Of course. We're all working on the same side of the curtain."

García kept staring at him. The gringo's smile turned less touristy, colder.

"Fact is," García said, "I haven't seen your credentials."

"True. Nor I yours."

"You've already investigated me. You should know me by now."

"Here." Graves took out a metal badge and a card. García looked them over carefully.

"Everything alright?"

"Yes."

"So, back to what we were talking about—our Russian colleague."

"He's already been investigated, hasn't he?"

"It's not so easy. Ivan Mikhailovich Laski took part in the

Spanish Civil War. Later, his name turns up in Asia, Central Europe, and Latin America. He speaks many languages without an accent, and there are long periods of time when he disappears altogether. For example, we haven't heard anything about him since 1960. He was in Cuba."

Graves spoke Spanish perfectly, without an accent. Fucking gringo! I bet the Russian'll give me the same line about this fellow. They've got people to investigate everything. I think that's all they do, investigate, and that's why they couldn't prevent what happened in Dallas. They were so busy investigating, they didn't see that guy with his rifle. And now, if we keep spinning our wheels, the same thing'll happen here while they're still investigating everybody. Who knows what he knows about me. For all I know he knows what a chump I was with Marta and that's why he's laughing so much. She looked so lovely, sleeping there in my bed. I would have liked to take her to Chapultepec Park today. Fucking Outer Mongolia!

"Based on our research, Mr. García, we have concluded that you have never been a Communist and that you once foiled a plot by Castro. That's why we consider you trustworthy."

Trustworthy with a gun, trustworthy to kill. How many Christian souls has this gringo sent on their way?

Graves stared intensely at him.

"You are anti-Communist, aren't you?"

"Didn't you just say you investigated me?"

"But you are anti-Communist?"

"I'm Mexican, and here in Mexico we have the freedom to be what the hell we want."

Fucking gringo! Why is it whenever you talk to one of them, you always end up making stupid speeches? Here we're all free to be whatever we are—fucking assembly lines of dead bodies, second-rate stiffs. And there are other people out there, out in

Outer Mongolia, people who have the freedom to churn out a load of first-rate dead people, proper corpses. Nothing better for that than Communists and anti-Communists. What if I tell him the truth? That I'm a hit man, a gunslinger, and that's that. And I don't give a damn what party the deceased belongs to. I even killed a priest once. Orders from General Marchena, back around '29.

Graves looked at him, his eyes steely, but with that same smile of a tourist, or maybe a used-car salesman.

"I thought we were going to collaborate, Mr. García."

"We are."

"So, do we agree on the tactic we'll use with our Russian colleague?"

"We'll see."

"I've told you everything we've done till now," Graves sounded offended. "You have contacts in the Chinese community, but you haven't told me anything."

"Nope."

"Do you actually have those contacts?"

"I play poker with them."

"Great contact."

Yeah, real great, for loosing money like a chump. Maybe this gringo, with his chronic investigationitis can be useful. Fucking Chinamen! Liu must be looking for Marta. Unless they were the ones who sent her to get me to my place and keep me distracted.

"There are indications that the Chinese know something, Graves."

"Really. That could be important."

"There's a Chinaman named Wang, owner of a joint on Donceles Street, Café Canton. You wouldn't be wasting your time if you investigated him."

He took a piece of paper out of his coat pocket that really look like a doctor's prescription, and at the bottom, written a different hand: "Someone's been tailing you since you left nborns." García didn't even twitch.

"I think that medicine will be good for you, if you take it with ot of milk. Me, I always drink coffee …"

"Last night at Café Canton you were drinking beer and that n be bad for you, García, my friend, very bad."

"What, the beer or Café Canton?"

"Both, as far as I could see."

"I, on the other hand, didn't see you drinking your milk."

The Russian smiled beatifically. Then he said:

"It does me good to go for a walk after I drink my milk. How bout we take a turn down the Alameda?"

"Let's."

Along the way they barely spoke. This fucking Russian didn't hug me like the gringo. I don't know what kind of a gun he's packing or what other arsenal he's carrying around. He's very clever, knows everything I'm up to. If I don't watch out, they'll start investigating the inside of my belly button. Fucking international conspiracy! But in this business, like in everything, you've got to stay alert—if you snooze you lose. Maybe that's why we sleep so little. Or because of our faithful departed. That's what the lay-sisters and the priests say, that our faithful departed don't let us sleep. Or, like the corrido says: *On my way through the graveyard / a dead man spoke to me; / hand me your skull, he cried / then alone I will not be.* Fucking corrido! For all I know those Outer Mongolians worry about the same things. I wonder what Chinese skulls look like? Very smiling. And that Russian knowing about me and Marta. And now he's acting all high and mighty with me.

"Why?"

"They say he supports Mao. And that he's organizing something."

Graves stood up and walked over to the telephone. Fucking FBI! All you got to do is mention Mao's name and they run off to report and investigate. Not bad, though, working with them. Here I sit, nice and easy, handing them information for them to investigate. It's like I'm the colonel. Maybe they'll even turn up something about Wang that I can use later. Those Chinamen always have dough and Yuan doesn't like him. There's got to be something to it. Fucking Chinamen. This gringo seems to know his trade. Very professional, karate, the whole enchilada. Marta should be up by now? After we meet with the Russian, I'm going to go buy her a dress and a coat. But maybe not, not yet. Who knows, maybe she can already see what a chump I am. And maybe this gringo is finking on me to the colonel or even del Valle, telling them I'm not playing nice. And me, I still can't figure out what Marta's up to. And now that I've got the gringo following a scent, I'd better play it cool. First I'll talk to the Russian, alone. For sure he'll feed me the same line as this one. All of them so professional and Marta making a chump out of me.

Graves returned and sat down:

"We'll have all the information we need in two hours. Where should we meet, Mr. García?"

"Do you know La Ópera cantina on Cinco de Mayo?"

"Sure do."

"At two?"

"Good. So, we have an understanding, Mr. García. You and I make one group, and the Russian makes another, if you know what I mean. We don't need to confide in him all our virgin experiences. Ha ha."

"No need to confide in anyone, Graves."

"I mean between you and me . . ."

"I understood. At two at La Ópera."

García stood up. Graves remained seated, still smiling, his eyes hard. He has false teeth. For all I know he'll pull a miniature gun out of one molar and a radio transmitter out of another, like in the movies they show on TV. Fucking gringos! Good thing I didn't tell him anything about last night. I definitely smell a rat there. If Luciano Manrique, or whatever the hell the name of the one with the bat was, had really wanted to kill me, he would have packed a gun or, at least, a knife. As I see it, they just wanted to give me a scare. But they ended up getting it. No, I don't think those guys were there to kill me. They were just delivering a message, letting me know they knew what I was up to. And if that's the case, then one of those Chinamen sent them. Or sent Marta to set me up. That means they do know. Or they think I'm on one job when I'm really on another. Like those guys tailing me, very professionally, as if they really knew what's what. Maybe they belong to the gringo or the Russian. Or the Chinese. At least these guys seem like they've got more know-how than the ones last night, who were complete and total morons.

He arrived at Café Paris, sat at a table facing the door, and ordered an espresso. It was a quarter to twelve. A shoeshine boy polished his shoes until they were shining like mirrors. He read the morning paper. There'll be something about the dead bodies in *Últimas Noticias* and *El Gráfico*. Another crime the police never manage to solve. But we're playing pretty rough with the cops. Maybe the colonel will tell them something to tide them over. Fucking colonel! Don't you go around killing people, García. So, why hire *me*? So I can submit six copies of a spiffed-up report? How many more are involved in this busi-

ness, anyway? For all I know, I'll end up [...] his pals. Things can get ugly when there's [...] prefer the old-fashioned way any day. Take t[...] off those guys, they're causing trouble. Non[...] Outer Mongolia or Hong Kong. And that [...] gullible and too friendly. That business of sm[...] it must be the latest fad. Like that gringo. But r[...] doesn't suit me, and anyway, only morons walk[...] all the time. What's to laugh about in this god[...] life? So del Valle doesn't like to talk to gunsling[...] ing to get to make his stiffs for him? And who'[...] Mexicans for a job like that? I don't think tho[...] night were martyrs for any Chinese Communi[...] one's dealing out some dough. A whole lot of [...] these things cost a pretty penny. Wouldn't be a [...] out who's got it and where it is. A few extra pesos[...] Hey, then I can spend them on Marta like a god[...]

At twelve sharp, a short thin man entered the c[...] like a nobody and was wearing a thick brown wo[...] tailored. He sat at the bar and ordered a glass of[...] stood up and went over to him:

"What's up?"

The man turned slowly, both hands resting on[...] had large blue eyes, surprisingly full of innocence.

"García!"

"What're you up to, Laski, my friend?"

"Having a glass of milk. At this time of day, my stor[...] acting up and milk settles it down."

"You don't say!"

"I went to the doctor and he gave me a prescriptio[...] look, García."

They sat down on a bench on the Alameda. The Russian chose one without a back where nobody could get near them without first being seen. He crossed his hands over his lap and contemplated the trees. García said:

"Seems you know everything, don't you?"

"Don't I?"

"How'd it go for you guys during the Spanish Civil War? Took quite a beating, didn't you?"

The Russian burst out laughing. His eyes shone with delight. He slapped García on the back several times:

"You'll make me die laughing, García. You are a man after my own heart. After everything that happened last night, you've still got jokes to tell. Wonderful, wonderful."

The Russian was laughing like a schoolboy. Here's another one who's got the giggles. Seems like in the international crowd, smiles are all the rage. We'll have to see if they'd keep laughing with a bullet in their bellies. Or when the shit hits the fan. For all I know, they'll chicken out and piss their pants. For all I know this Russian would just keep laughing. Fucking Russian. The professor says that man doesn't laugh at death, that's what animals do. As if you can laugh at life.

The Russian said:

"Now, Mr. García, now that we've dispensed with the pleasantries, what do you say we talk about our case? You've met Graves. I can assure you, that American is one of the FBI's best agents. Don't let his stupid laugh and bourgeois appearance fool you. He's a very good agent and he never hesitates to kill when necessary. That's why I think you and I should form a united front, of sorts, and not tell him everything we find out. If you weren't going to tell him about last night, I won't, either."

"How much did you see?"

"Almost all of it. Once they told me I would have the honor of working with you, I took a room in the hotel across the street from your apartment. Routine stuff, Mr. García."

"Same routine stuff with Graves?"

"Naturally. And he with me, though I think last night he hadn't yet started his surveillance on you."

"How much did you see last night?"

"The one driving the Pontiac got quite a blow to the head."

"Maybe he was one of yours?"

The Russian looked surprised, and his eyes showed that he was offended.

"Oh, no. Those men were amateurs. We work only with professionals. The stupidest of my men would never have stuck his head out the window of a car so carelessly. I can assure you, they weren't Graves's men, either. He also only uses professionals."

"I see."

There was a certain sadness in Laski's voice, as well as a touch of scorn.

"As I said, they were amateurs."

"You know who they were?"

"I haven't wasted any time finding out. Early this morning I spoke to the police, told them there was a car parked on the street with two dead bodies. Probably in the afternoon papers I'll find out who they were."

"They were Mexicans."

Laski was quiet, thinking. The information surprised him. Finally I say something he doesn't already know. Aren't I hot shit! Did he see everything that went on with Marta? The curtain was open. Fucking Russian!

"This is important," said Laski, finally. "Very important. Are you sure that those two men, the one in the car and the one you brought down from your apartment wrapped in a sheet, are you sure they were involved?"

"Who's sure of anything?"

"That's why I'm asking. Given the international importance of this case, it seems very strange that two amateurs would be involved, on either side. See what I mean?"

"Yes."

"That's why it is essential to find out if their appearance last night was because of the case we are working on or something else, perhaps something personal against you, Mr. García."

"I'd never seen either of them before, and their names mean nothing to me, Mr. Laski. And they showed up the same night I begin on this investigation. Could be a coincidence, but I don't like coincidences."

"Last night was also the first time, I believe, you took the young lady to your house."

"What do you know about that?"

"This could be another coincidence. Miss Fong, lovely, indeed, shows up at your house with you. And two men who want to kill you also show up. Don't you think Miss Fong might be involved?"

"What do I know."

"Or the two dead men might have been after her, there to wrench her out of your arms, Mr. García. Maybe a jealous lover or boyfriend. Could that be?"

"Yeah, could be. But anyway, you're the ones who started this whole mess with your Outer Mongolian gossip."

"Would you have preferred we say nothing to your government? That would not have been a very friendly gesture on our part, especially when the life of your own president could be in danger."

His large blue eyes now showed that he was deeply offended, and somewhat sad. His nostrils quivered.

"We are grateful for your warning, Mr. Laski; and I imagine that the Americans are, too. Maybe this will put an end to the Cold War."

"The Cold War is a bourgeois invention."

"What I would like to point out, Laski, before you launch into any speeches, is that both you and Graves, instead of looking for the men who've come from Hong Kong, if they exist, are spending your time investigating and watching each other and me."

The Russian burst out laughing.

"Seems like a game, doesn't it? It's always like this when there's international intrigue."

"A game that could end, the day after tomorrow, with two dead presidents."

"We did our duty by issuing a warning as soon as we found out that something was going on, Mr. García."

"Precisely. And we've done our duty by thanking you. And now comes the million-dollar question: What interest do you, the Russians, have in continuing with the investigation?"

"A very good question, Mr. García. Very good."

"I'd like an answer that is just as good."

"But that would diminish the stature of such a question. A question like that deserves to remain forever unanswered. That's another thing about international intrigue: most questions remain unanswered."

"I'd like an answer anyway."

"Let's just say, we continue investigating out of curiosity, Mr. García. We Russians are sentimental, feminine in many respects, and therefore, curious."

The Russian's smile was beatific: it oozed innocence. This guy looks at me like I'm a real jackass. But even that doesn't make me want to smack him. It would be like smacking a child. For all I know he'll start crying. Fucking Russian! But sharp as a tack. Full of a whole lot of international intrigue. Him and the gringo combined, they'll investigate me down to my underwear. In the meantime, those Outer Mongolians, if they even exist, are preparing their sniper rifles with telescopic sights or their bomb or whatever they're going to use.

"You look deep in thought, García. Would you like to hear something else?"

"I want to know *something*, period."

"There's another rumor . . ."

"From Outer Mongolia? I guess they're carrying the rumors by camel, like the Three Kings."

"Very funny, García, my friend. I think we are going to understand each other quite well, quite well."

"So, the new rumor?"

"Somebody took out of Hong Kong Shanghai Bank, in Hong Kong, a half million dollars, all in fifty-dollar bills. American bills, that is. Not worth as much as the ruble, but still a large sum."

"Ten thousand bills. That's a hefty wad."

"Exactly. And it appears that these bills were on their way to Mexico."

"Interesting."

"But nobody has seen them on any border."

"There are many things that are never seen on any border, Mr. Laski."

"Very true, very true."

"You think that money is from Mr. Mao?"

"The People's Republic of China."

"Maybe it came directly from Moscow?"

"Maybe. China has cost us a lot of money. A lot."

"And now they're pissed at you."

"So it is."

"Ungrateful wretches!"

The Russian was thinking. In a nearby gazebo, the Chinese from Dolores Street had begun to assemble for their daily gathering. Santiago and Pedro Yuan are probably there. And here I am, playing at international intrigue. I smell a rat, but chances are these lofty political issues have already been checked out by the men at the top. Mr. Rosendo del Valle and his bigwigs. None of my business. My business is to make stiffs. Those bigwigs must know why the Russians are going around pointing fingers at the Chinese. But what I'd really like to find out is where the money is. That's a lot of dough. Find the guys who have it, take them out, keep the dough, as much as possible, and as they say on TV: mission accomplished. Fucking mission!

"So, Laski, my friend, you people think that dough is going to land here, in the hands of some Chinaman, who's going to use it to plan and carry out the attack."

"That's very possible."

"Have you got any solid evidence? And don't give me Outer Mongolia again, because by now I'm not even sure it exists ..."

"I've been there. As for your question, there might be no solid evidence, but it is logical. In these cases of international intrigue, there's never solid evidence or complete truths, García, my friend."

"What makes you think this money will land in the hands of a Chinaman and not somebody else?"

"The Chinese wouldn't trust that much money to anybody who wasn't Chinese."

"The Peking Communists, as they are called, have many followers all over the world. Some say they have more than you."

"University kids playing at being conspirators."

"I'm asking because if it turns out, as I think it will, that the two from last night were mixed up in this business, we've got two Mexicans who definitely weren't doing whatever they were doing out of some kind of political commitment. Which means the money has already arrived."

"And they're wasting it on amateurs."

Laski's big eyes filled with rage.

"And now, Laski, I'm going to ask you a question, and I hope you won't take offense. Might you be the one in charge of making sure this money doesn't get wasted?"

"I can assure you that if this were the case, the two men who died last night would never have been hired. Anything else?"

"Yes. How are we going to work together?"

"You and I ..."

"And Graves. Don't forget Graves, Laski."

"No, I never forget him. Where do you propose we start? You are, we could say, our host ..."

"I think we should start by finding out several things. First: if your government was pulling a fast one when they issued that noble and disinterested warning. Second: if those mysterious assassins from Hong Kong have arrived in Mexico. Third: if those half a million bucks have arrived and if they're going to be used to carry out the attack. Fourth: if the two men who died last night were involved in this."

"There are other questions, Mr. García, there are others. I would say, a fifth one would be: if Miss Fong, who was with you last night, is involved."

García's eyes turned hard, impenetrable. Laski kept talking, counting on his fingers:

"Sixth: if Miss Fong is an agent for one of the groups involved, how much power does she have over you, Mr. García? Don't you think it is important to thoroughly investigate that?"

"And seventh, Mr. Laski: if the illustrious government of the Union of Soviet Socialist Republics hasn't pulled the wool over our eyes with their Chinese and Outer Mongolian rumors, so that while we're trying to find the Chinese, the Russians can do what they say the Chinese want to do."

Laski clapped his hands in delight and again broke out in childish laughter.

"We're going to be friends, García, great friends. That's absolutely clear to me now. Can I call you Filiberto? My name is Ivan Mikhailovich."

"Fine by me, Ivan Mikhailovich, now that we've shared all our secrets and established such a close friendship, where do *you* propose we start?"

"It's your call, Filiberto."

"Of all the issues we've discussed, the only sure thing is that the two guys from last night are dead. We could start there."

"Okay. Let's find out if they were involved."

"I'll do that."

"As will we, Filiberto, as will we. I imagine our friend Graves is also interested, because by now he must know something about what happened last night."

"Good. And now for that beautiful question that has so far remained unanswered."

The expression on Laski's face was very serious.

"My government has certain differences of criteria with the government of the People's Republic of China. My government also wishes to maintain the current status of its relationship with the United States. Moreover, my government would not be upset if the relationship between the United States and the Chinese Republic deteriorated even further. As you can see, we are not now interested in the death of the president of the United States ..."

"But you are interested in the Chinese taking the blame for anything that might happen."

"You are distrustful, Filiberto."

"I have to be, Ivan Mikhailovich."

"Where do you want to meet at seven this evening?"

"Café Canton."

"You think that's a good idea?"

"We've got to shake things up, Laski. We've got to see how those Chinamen react."

"Perhaps you are right. We'll meet there, Filiberto. I will bring those who are following me and you will bring those who are following you. By the way, do you know if your government has ordered that I be watched?"

García smiled.

"See you later, Ivan Mikhailovich."

The Russian started walking toward El Caballito. A man sitting on a bench and reading a newspaper a little ways away stood up and started walking toward El Caballito. García turned toward Cinco de Mayo and a man was soon tailing him from a distance. It would be easy to lose him, but what's the point. That fucking Russian knows everything. Like the gringo. Even Marta's name. How did he find out? For all I know Marta is working for him.

He stopped at a tobacconist and made a phone call:

"Marta?"

"Is that you, Filiberto? I read your note and ... thank you, thank you so much, but I can't stay here ..."

"It's your home, Marta. I offer it to you with all my heart."

"Thank you. You've been so good to me that … that I want to cry like a fool."

"Has anybody called, Marta?"

"No."

"I'm going to try to stop by this afternoon so we can talk. See you then, Marta, and in the meantime, behave yourself … almost."

Before hanging up he could hear Marta giggling. Just hearing her laugh gives me knots in my stomach. That damn Marta, she's so fine. And that fucking Russian! Who's he playing for a fool? Am I really behaving like a snot-nosed kid with my first girlfriend? And Marta looking at my mug, my stupid mug, while I say: "Consider this your home, Marta." "You sleep in the bed, I'll sleep here in the living room." And her in the bed, looking so virginal. For all I know that Chinaman Liu already had the pleasure. And all I got was a peck on the cheek. With such pretty lips. And to think, I've never done it with a Chinese gal. So, what if I am a chump. Fuck that Russian and his god-damned gossip! Maybe he's right and I should investigate her. I'd do better to investigate between her legs. Word about me and Marta must've already reached Outer Mongolia. Fucking Outer Mongolia!

He dialed another number:

"García here, Colonel."

"Killed somebody else?"

"I made the contacts. Can you tell me if Roque Villegas had any dollars on him?"

"He did."

"In fifty-dollar bills?"

"Yes. Thirty bills. That is, if the ambulance people didn't pocket a few."

"All fifties?"

"Yes. Why?"

"I think we're starting to get somewhere. Do you have Villegas's address, Colonel?"

"He lived with a woman he brought here from Tijuana, a gringa. At 208 Guerrero, apartment 9."

"Did you already talk to her?"

"No, I haven't wanted her to know anything yet. I want to see what she'll do."

"I'm going to go see her."

"I don't want that gringa ending up dead, García."

"I'll do my best, Colonel."

He hung up the phone, then made his way to La Ópera cantina. He went all the way to the booths in the back, where bold and veiled women used to sit in the old days; now, there are only men seeking even more solitude than what they carry around with them. He sat down and ordered some *tacos de ubre* and a beer. Fucking colonel! He doesn't want the gringa ending up dead. I don't give a damn if she's dead or alive. What do I care about any of it. Outer Mongolia and the Russians and the gringo president. What the fuck do I care about it! And all that crap about my loyalty to the government—what has the government ever done for me? Fucking salary they pay me! And if you don't stay on your toes, with the government or without it, you'll be down on your knees, with your loyalty or without it. A lot of fifty-dollar bills are floating around out there. Ten thousand of them.

"What's up, Cap'n?"

"How's it going, Professor? Won't you have a tequila?"

The professor sat down across from him, the marble of the table top between them. His age, like the color of his suit, was indefinite. The few shy and yellowed teeth he still had appeared every once in a while behind his smile, which was also shy. A tie, also of indefinite color, hung from his thin neck. His shirt was old and dirty. His hands, when he brought the glass of tequila to his lips, were trembling.

"You didn't come last night, Cap'n. We needed one more for dominoes."

"No. I didn't come."

"Work or pleasure?"

"To your health, Professor."

"A fellow came around looking for you."

"You don't say."

"Said he was a friend. He stood me two drinks, there, at the bar."

"Really!"

"I didn't know him, Cap'n, but he didn't fool me. I told him you always drank tequila and he said, yeah, that you were quite the tequila drinker."

The professor emptied his glass. García ordered him another. Those guys came all the way here looking for me?

"What time was that?"

"Around nine."

They brought the tequila and the *tacos de ubre*.

"You don't want any?"

"No thanks, Cap'n. I eat lunch later ... when I eat at all. Cheers."

He emptied his glass. Or maybe the professor is telling me tales so he can mooch more tequilas. Fucking professor!

"So, then what happened?"

"Look, Cap'n, when someone comes in here asking for a man like you and says he's a friend, a bosom buddy, and he doesn't even know that you never drink tequila, there's something fishy going on. Could it be the cops?"

"Anybody's guess."

"When he left, I followed him a little, but then I lost him on Donceles. That is, I ran into Ibarrita and he bought me a tequila ..."

"Was he Mexican?"

"Yeah. Dressed like a *pocho*, but definitely Mexican. About my height, more Indian looking. And he was carrying a gun under his armpit."

"Sure you don't want some tacos, Professor?"

"Rather have another tequila."

García ordered him another tequila. Based on his description, that was Roque Villegas. There's me figuring he'd been following me since Dolores, and it turns out he came here looking for me. And now he's not looking for me anywhere. Fucking stiff! And the other, Luciano Manrique, he knew I hung out on Dolores with the Chinamen. This is getting very complicated.

"Listen, Professor, want to do me a favor and earn a few bucks?"

"Do I have to kill anybody?"

"No, just defend a widow."

"A do-it-yourself widow or you lent a hand?"

"Not exactly a widow. They weren't married."

"A mistress."

"Yeah, they killed her lover."

"You did?"

"Yeah. And the man was carrying fifteen-hundred dollars in his pocket, in fifty-dollar bills."

"And you left them where they were, Cap'n?"

"The police have them. I want you to pay a visit to the woman; she still doesn't know he's dead ..."

"What? You think she has more of the same?"

"I don't know. Tell her you'll represent her, that you'll help her get back that money that is rightfully hers."

"That's true. The law protects ..."

"She's a gringa."

"Even more reason. A woman alone, in a foreign land, her husband deceased ..."

"Save the demagoguery for her, Professor. What I want is for you to go and tell her you can get her the money, for a commission ..."

"Fifty percent?"

"Ten ..."

"That's low."

"Anyway, you're not going to get the money. That's why I'm paying you ..."

"But she can, legally, claim that money ..."

"I don't give a shit about that, Professor. What I want to know is where the money came from, who gave it to Villegas ..."

"Villegas, Cap'n? Would that be Roque Villegas?"

"Yeah."

"It was in the afternoon paper ..."

"You'll tell the woman that you have to show where the money came from in order to get it back. In other words, that she has to prove that it really belonged to Villegas ..."

"Understood."

"I'll arrive while you're with her. Pretend you don't know me, but play along. By the time I get there, I want her to know everything and be real eager to get that money back."

"What do I get out of it, Cap'n?"

"Two hundred pesos."

"Three hundred. I have to pay my room ..."

"Two hundred."

"Okay. Where does she live?"

"At 208 Guerrero, apartment 9."

"I'll go tomorrow."

"You'll go now. I'll arrive at four."

"But ..."

"Now."

"Give me something for the cab."

He gave him ten pesos. The professor took the money, which vanished in his hands as if by magic.

"Okay, I'm going."

"Those ten are on account."

"Don't be so hard on me, Cap'n. A man's gotta live ..."

The professor left the cantina. Thirty of the ten thousand bills have shown up. I'd like to find myself a bundle. Could be that my friend Ivan Mikhailovich saw what a chump I am. Like Marta. And it'll turn out there's no ten thousand fifty-dollar bills and there's no Marta. Fucking Marta! For all I know Liu knocked her up. And me playing the soap opera. Fucking Palmolive! If only Ramona from Chiapas could've seen me: "Fili darling, you'd hump a pole if it had an ass." That's what that bitch would say. And all because I broke in the servant at the whorehouse. Somebody had to start her off. And that other one, in Veracruz: "For you, love is jumping on top of a woman. I think for you a woman is just a hole with legs." So, what else is a bitch for? Straight to business. Just like with the dead. Why beat around the bush? The dead in the ground and the man in the bitch. Why the prologue? Slam, bam. With bitches and with the dead. It's the same shit. All the rest is decoration, for perverts. And now here I am with my, "You can sleep in the bedroom, dear Marta." Maybe I can't get it up anymore and that's why I'm acting so paternal. Fucking Marta! Mother fucker! I'm going to talk to the gringo, then go straight home. And that'll be the end of the soap opera, and on to the only thing that matters. You,

Marta, get in bed, and me with you. But she's not that type. Then what good is she? Maybe I'll bring her flowers. There I go, back to the soaps! And then there was that day I brought flowers, in Parral. I wasn't going to sleep with Jacinta Ricarte. The flowers were for her grave. I was dead drunk and Sergeant Garrido nabbed me. I didn't have orders to kill Jacinta Ricarte. Fucking flowers! And here that gringo is about to tell me he knows everything, just like the Russian.

Graves entered the cantina flourishing his smile in style. He was carrying a black leather briefcase under his arm. When he saw García, his smile shined even more brightly. That gringo acts like he wants to sell me something real bad. For all I know he's a faggot and he's taken a shine to me.

"My good friend García."

"What's up?"

Graves sat down across from him.

"You've eaten?

"Yes, of course. We eat lunch at noon; it gives us a long afternoon to work."

"Want some coffee?"

"Would they have American coffee?"

"Maybe."

They brought him a big cup with some coffee and hot water. Graves tasted it, then didn't touch it again.

"That's what happens to me in Sanborns when I order coffee," García said.

Graves smiled.

"Doesn't matter. I ordered it to keep you company."

"Want a cognac?"

"No, thank you. Not when I'm working. García, I know Laski has men tailing me."

"And you've got men tailing him."

"That's routine. But there are others, I don't think they're Laski's. Are they yours?"

"And there are others tailing me, too. Laski's, yours, and others. We're a proper procession."

"You don't know who those others might belong to?"

"Mr. Mao?"

"You sure?"

"No. You?"

"If they're tailing us, we must be onto something."

"Look, Graves, how about we cut the crap? If you and Laski would use your people for something more useful, we might be able to find out who those others are."

Graves laughed.

"Right you are, García, my friend. But we'd have to make a deal with Laski, who is a very dangerous man. Though sometimes I think we carry our distrust a little too far."

"Like I said."

"For example, you didn't mention a word about your activities last night, and if it hadn't been because I took the precaution of putting surveillance on you from the start, I wouldn't have known anything. That is not okay, García. We agreed to cooperate."

"Are you sure what happened last night has something to do with our investigation?"

Graves was busy lighting a cigarette. The next time I pick up a Chinese gal, I'll just take her to the Olympic Stadium, there'd be fewer people there. If I'd known, I would've sold tickets.

"The incident," Graves said, "started in Café Canton, which you asked me to investigate."

"So?"

"A Pontiac began to follow you from there, the same Pontiac in which, this morning, two dead bodies were found."

"Are you sure they're involved?"

"It adds up, unless you asked me to investigate Wang from Café Canton for some other reason?"

Graves's voice was hard. In spite of his smile, you could tell he was not amused.

"We are dealing here with a very serious matter. The life of the president of the United States of America, and maybe even world peace, hangs in the balance. And we have very little time …"

"So, stop wasting it telling me off and tell me what you found out from Wang."

Graves smiled. He placed his briefcase on the table but didn't open it. Now he'll pull out a stack of papers. A thousand-page investigation. Give 'em to your fucking mother to read.

"Wang imports merchandise from Communist China through Hong Kong. Mostly canned Chinese food. He brings in a significant amount of merchandise. The last shipment was worth eighty thousand pesos. I think the Mexican police should search the café and his warehouses in Nonoalco."

"Looking for what? Canned lard and fish sauce? My government doesn't prohibit trade with China."

"This is a special case."

"Anyway, I found out that there are half a million dollars in fifty-dollar bills, out there, floating around, as we say, somewhere."

"How do you know, García?"

"The money comes from Hong Kong. With half a million dollars you can get a pope assassinated, never mind a president."

"How did you find out about that money?"

"Maybe your people, who like to investigate so much, would have news of an operation of that magnitude. The money, in cash, comes from Hong Kong Shanghai Bank, in Hong Kong."

"Yesterday Wang exchanged, at Banco Nacional, a hundred fifty-dollar bills. He changed them for pesos."

"Graves, you think you can get the numbers of the bills from the Hong Kong bank?"

"I can try, through London, but we don't have much time."

"Do it, even if you have to go through Outer Mongolia. And we've got a date, at seven, at Café Canton, with Laski."

"Okay. What was that you said about Outer Mongolia?"

"Nothing. It was a joke. See you at seven."

García stood up. Graves stayed seated:

"I'd like to know where you get your information, García. About the money."

"You would?"

"It's important."

"One of the dead men in the Pontiac was carrying thirty fifty-dollar bills. A lot of dough for a guy like that."

"Half a million dollars is too much money for something like this, García."

"You don't think your president's life is worth that much?"

"These kinds of attacks are usually carried out by fanatics, people who don't need to get paid much. Half a million is a lot of money."

"See you at seven."

García went out and stopped at a public telephone.

"García here, Colonel."

"Kill anybody else?"

"Have you got those bills they found on Villegas?"

"Yes. And they're staying right here."

"I just want the numbers."

The colonel told him the numbers and García jotted them down on an old envelope.

"Thanks, Colonel."

"The person we talked to last night called me. He wants a report."

"Okay."

"You've got nothing more to say?"

"Could you also get the numbers of some fifty-dollar bills that Wang, from Café Canton, changed at the Banco Nacional? There were a hundred of them."

"Yeah, that's easy. The bank has no reason to conceal that information. You can ask them yourself."

"I don't have time. The president of the United States arrives tomorrow."

"Keep me informed."

The colonel hung up. Fucking colonel and his jokes! Have I killed anybody else. What does he care, as long as I don't kill his clients? They've all gotten so high and mighty. Like that del Valle. Who said anything about killing anybody? And me still in the same old shit—but now it's even worse. There used to be respect. I was Filiberto García, the man who killed Teódulo Reina in Irapuato. When that fucking little colonel was a nobody, a punk kid. But it's not like that now, now the Revolution wears white gloves. And that gringo asks too many questions. Same as the Russian. All this shit about investigating, about being a team. Fucking team! These things are done by one man, alone. Filiberto García, who killed Teódulo Reina in Irapuato. Alone. Man to man. No investigation needed. Fucking colonel!

He tried to catch a taxi, but couldn't, and ended up taking a bus. Guerrero Street, number 208, was an ugly apartment building, the kind of ugly reserved for this street. Apartment

9 was on the second floor, at the end of a filthy hallway with paint peeling off walls where several generations of renters had scrawled their ideas about politics, life, death, and, above all, sex. García stopped and rang the bell. It didn't seem to be working, so he knocked. A few moments later the door opened. A blond woman dressed in a dirty bathrobe, her hair mussed and her face smeared with traces of yesterday's makeup, spoke to him in English, then sprinkled it with Spanish:

"*What the hell ... ?*"

"Police."

He showed her a badge. The woman brought her hand to her mouth, as if to stifle a shout, and let him in. He entered a room filled with a motley collection of old, cheap furniture. Disorder reigned. The dining table was strewn with dirty dishes and the floor with newspapers, cigarettes butts, and items of clothing. On a couch in the middle of that mess sat the professor, a cup in his hand and a bottle of rum on the coffee table in front of him. The professor stood up.

"Police," García said to him.

"I am a lawyer and I represent this woman."

The woman stood absolutely still next to the open door, her hand over her mouth, still struggling to stifle that shout. García turned to her:

"Are you the wife of Roque Villegas Vargas?"

"Yes, I am. And the money he was carrying is mine ... mine. *The dirty bum, the lowdown dirty bastard ...* That money is mine ..."

The professor walked across the room and closed the door. The woman kept talking:

"That money is mine ... it's all mine and don't think for a minute I'm going to let you cops steal it from me."

"Mr. Policeman," the professor interrupted, "this woman has

just now found out about the death of Mr. Villegas Vargas ..."

"The dirty bum, the no-good motherfucking bastard—"

"... and naturally she is quite upset by the news."

"I want that money, all of it—"

"On the other hand, I have recommended she take a bit of a stimulant, a sip of rum, to perhaps calm her frayed nerves—"

"The no-good sonofabitch. One thousand five hundred bucks, Mr. Policeman, and they're mine ... all mine."

García stood there staring at her. The woman closed her mouth, which she had readied for further expressions of her sorrow, and took a step back.

"Do you have any documents that prove you are Villegas Vargas's legal spouse?"

The professor intervened:

"Look, Mr. Policeman—"

The woman gestured to him to shut up:

"That money is mine. It's the only damn thing I'm going to get out of this whole fucking mess, five months living with that *motherfucking bastard* ... The only—"

"Do you have any documents?"

The professor again intervened:

"She has her passport, and everything is in order. She is in Mexico legally ..."

"She is, eh?"

"Now, sir, one minor—let us say—legal requirement does seem to be missing—the marriage license. But, as you know, our laws are compassionate and protect mistresses in good standing. It can be proven beyond reasonable doubt that this woman has lived with Mr. Villegas Vargas as his wife and, hence, has full rights to the estate left by the deceased—"

"You tell him, Mr. Lawyer! Damn right I have my rights ...

That money is mine, and if you steal it from me, I'll go straight to my consulate. No goddamned *greaser* is going to take it away from me. A thousand five hundred dollars. *Holy Jesus!*"

"It is true, Mr. Policeman. She is under the protection not only of our humanitarian laws but also the government of the United States of America."

"Identification, please," García demanded from the woman.

She ran into the other room and returned almost instantaneously with an enormous, flaming-red handbag. She opened it, dug around inside, and pulled out an American passport. She held it out to García triumphantly and with absolute confidence. Just seeing her passport infused her with renewed strength, as if it placed her in a different human category.

"Look, *American Citizen.* See. *Anabella Ninziffer, from Wichita Falls, theater artist.* And look at my tourist card. Everything's in order. Everything—"

"I see."

"Obviously, I don't use my real name on stage and in cabarets. My stage name is Anabella Crawford. Maybe you've seen me advertised in Tijuana or maybe L.A."

García handed her back her passport. Fucking gringa! Her mouth stinks like a cantina at daybreak. Big deal, an American citizen, like that'd be enough to scare me off.

"*Look here, mister ... I'm telling you, that money's mine ...*"

"We'll see."

"*Come on, honey. Be good ...* Be good with me and *I'll be good with you*? Want to come to a *party* tonight, just you by your lonesome? ... I've always liked strong dark men with green eyes. *I'll be good, honey.*"

The professor poured himself another glass of rum and drank it down in one gulp. Anabella sidled up to García, letting her robe open at her neckline. Under her robe, there was only Anabella, lots of Anabella.

"I haven't done no deal with this shyster ... with this lawyer. He wanted some of my money, *honey.*"

"Really?"

"He wanted thirty percent of my money. *Five hundred dollars. Jesus F. Christ!* Ain't it true I don't got to give him nothing? You're going to get it for me, aren't you?"

"If you can prove where that money came from, there's no reason you have to give anything to anybody."

"What?"

García repeated the sentence, this time in English. The woman kept talking, also in English:

"He earned it, every penny of it. We both earned it ..."

"What kind of work did he do?"

"He was hired, for a special job, an investigation. He was a private detective, honey."

"Who hired him?"

"That car's mine too, the Pontiac. I gave him the money to buy it in Tijuana."

"Who hired him?"

"You gotta give me that money, and the car, too. It's all mine ..."

"Who hired him?"

The woman went over to the table, picked up the bottle of rum, and took a huge slug.

"Honey, you don't need to know that. Come back tonight and you'll see that none of that matters ... We'll have a party ..."

García went straight up to her. His eyes were two chunks of green ice. With his left hand he yanked the bottle away from her and with the left he gave her a sharp slap.

"Who hired him?"

The woman brought her hands to her mouth. Her eyes were spinning. She slowly sank into an armchair, still not removing her hands from her mouth. The tears welled up in her eyes, then rolled down her cheeks, mixing with mascara and powder.

"Who hired him?"

"I can't ... I can't tell you. I can't. But that money's mine, it's all I've got ... I've got nothing else. That bastard took everything from me. In Tijuana he said ... I was a performer there ... He said we were going to make a bundle ..."

"Who with?"

"I can't ... I can't tell you ... I'm afraid."

García grabbed her robe and pulled her up to standing. Anabella's eyes looked like they were going to pop out of her head. Her full lips were trembling.

"They were Chinamen who hired him, weren't they?"

The woman shook her head, weakly.

"Wang, from Café Canton, right?"

The woman kept shaking her head. García let go of her robe and pushed her into the chair. Anabella covered her face with her hands and began sobbing.

"We can have a party, honey ... A really good party. Tonight."

"Was it Wang?"

Anabella nodded.

"What was the job?"

"I don't know ... I don't know ... Something very secret, very mysterious. They didn't want to tell me anything ... Rock, that's how I called Roque, he promised me we were going to have lots of money and be very important ... But I don't know what the job was."

García turned, as if to leave.

"But, Mr. Policeman ... Mister ... you promised you'd get me that money ... And the car ..."

"Talk to your lawyer."

"That crummy bastard! Best you come back tonight, at nine, I'll explain everything to you. I'll spiff myself up and we'll have a party. You want a party with an American girl, eh, lover boy?"

García left, closing the door behind him. Fucking washed-up gringa! Still reeking of the rotgut she drank last night. I'd almost rather sleep with the professor. So Wang was going around dealing out the dough, eh? Those fucking Chinamen. Now they're really in for it. And the guys from Communist China trying to play catch-up in this international intrigue. Just look at how they're fucking it up! That's why I smell a goddamned rat here. Fucking rat! All that bullshit about Outer Mongolia, and this is all they can come up with. And out there are a bunch of fifty-dollar bills, greenbacks. I could buy Marta a fur coat. There I go, acting like a chump again. No. Tonight, she either gives out or she gets out. She's too damn fine. Half a million for a fuck-up like this? More than six million pesos. Wait till the colonel hears. Then we'll start the game of marbles—who's got their marbles? And who's lost theirs. Whoever takes the first turn usually wins, and that'll be me.

IV

When García opened the door to his apartment, Marta was on the floor on her knees, cleaning the rug with a damp rag. She looked up when she heard the door open:

"The stain is almost gone, Filiberto."

"Why are you doing this, Marta?"

Marta stood up slowly.

"I thought you wouldn't be back till late, and I didn't have anything else to do."

"Have you eaten, Marta?"

"I made a little rice."

"That's all?"

"I'm not hungry, Filiberto."

García closed the door, walked into the bedroom, and took off his hat. Marta kept looking down at the rug she'd been cleaning. When García returned, she lifted her eyes to look at him.

"What happened?"

"No big deal, Marta."

"But, those men . . ."

"They were both criminals, wanted by the police."

He sat down on the sofa. Maybe she'll come sit next to me and I'll put my arm around her. I should have put my arms around her when I came in. I'm really turning into a faggot.

Marta took the rag into the kitchen. From there she called out:

"Do you want some coffee? I made some ..."

"Thanks, Marta, but you shouldn't bother ..."

"I'll bring it to you. Do you want some cognac?"

"Yes ... please."

"Coming."

Marta's voice sounded happy, confident. She's not afraid like she was last night. Maybe now she'll play harder to get. She didn't try to kiss me when I came in, didn't even give me her hand. I made her not afraid of me and now she brushes me off. That's what I get for being a dumbass—and a faggot. I'm a fucking faggot.

Marta returned from the kitchen and placed the coffee and the cognac on the coffee table. Then she sat down next to him.

"I put in sugar. One spoonful, the way you like it."

"Thank you, Marta."

He took a sip of the coffee. Just like I like it. What I like is her, but I sit here playing the chump.

"Want some cognac?"

"Thank you, Marta."

She poured some cognac into a glass. Thank you, Marta. Seems like that's all I know how to say, like a schoolboy.

"Cheers, Marta. Won't you have a glass with me?"

"No, thank you, Filiberto. Truth is, I don't like cognac."

"What do you like to drink, Marta?"

"Nothing. Sometimes a little wine, but I prefer not to drink anything. I also cleaned your suit ... from last night, and washed your shirt."

"You shouldn't have bothered, Marta."

"I thought it wouldn't be a good idea to give it to the cleaners. Then people start talking. But you say there's no danger..."

"No, none at all, Marta. And now I'm going to go see a lawyer about getting your birth certificate. Marta Fong García's. For all we know, I'm your uncle, Marta."

"At least poor Alicia Fong's."

"That's you now, forever. And more Mexican than *chilaquiles*. Here's to you, my fellow Mexican."

Marta lowered her head. When she looked up, there were tears in her eyes. She gave him a kiss on the cheek:

"Thank you, Filiberto, thank you so much."

"Don't mention it, Marta."

Marta stood up and walked over to the open window. She spoke from there, her voice full of feeling:

"So, I'm no longer in danger, I'll never be in danger, and I'll never again be afraid. You probably think I'm foolish, but I've lived with this fear for so many years that it's going to take me a while to get used to not carrying it around all the time. I'm going to have to get used to facing life head on, looking people straight in the eye, not hiding, as I've always done."

"Nobody can do anything to you anymore, Marta."

"I'm free ... I have to get used to this, to being free. I have to say it, over and over again. I won't have to work for whatever they want to pay me. And I'm never going back to Mr. Liu's house..."

"I thought he was your guardian, Marta."

Marta didn't answer. García stood up and went into the bedroom. Fucking faggot! I didn't take advantage of her when she was afraid and now I'm not taking advantage of her when she's grateful. Maybe that Russian's got me all tied up in knots, because I know he's watching everything. I should close the curtain. Fucking Russian! I should bring her in here, into bed, and go for it. Cut to the goddamned chase.

He walked back to the door between the bedroom and the living room. Marta was standing up, looking at him.

"All of this is thanks to you, Filiberto."

"It has been my pleasure."

"I knew you were good. A man that makes a girl like me, a nobody, laugh, like you do, has to be good."

"Don't say that, Marta."

García went into the bathroom and closed the door. Now I'm really fucked. Even my voice is coming out all shaky and weak. Next I'll start bawling like an old woman. Or like a faggot. Anyway, they say that men, when they get old, turn into faggots.

He washed his hands and came out of the bathroom. Marta was still standing there, at the door.

"I knew I wasn't wrong to tell you all that, Filiberto. And that's why I want to tell you the rest."

García's eyes turned cold, calculating. Now the truth will come out. All she had to do was see my dumbass face, and she's out of here. But if that's where she's heading, she'll put out or she'll put out, period, even if the Russian does see the whole thing. Fucking Russian! For all I know he's listening, too. He probably put microphones everywhere. But the Russian can go fuck himself. She's going to have to put out.

"Come here, Filiberto ... Sit down, on the sofa."

García sat down. She kneeled in front of him, on the floor, looking up at him from below. Her eyes were filled with tears.

"I didn't want to Filiberto, I swear, I didn't, but I was Mr. Liu's mistress. His second wife, he called me. I didn't want to, but I was so afraid. And then I got used to it. I thought it was going to go on forever, for my whole life. He came to my room every Tuesday and Saturday night. His wife, the poor thing, she knew everything, but he says those things don't matter, that's the Chinese custom. And his wife is afraid of him, too. She and I, we've always done whatever he wanted. We never dared disobey him. He doesn't think there's anything wrong with what he did, but I think there is ... But I couldn't do anything to stop him, and twice a week I had to wait for him in my room."

"Why are you telling me this, Marta?"

"Because you've been so good to me ... Like a father, like more than a father. Ever since I left the nuns in Macao, nobody has ever been kind to me. But you are, and you haven't asked for anything in return ..."

She threw her arms around him and started to cry on his shoulder. Like a father. Fucking father! If she only knew what I'm going to ask her for. But that Chinaman Liu already beat me to it. Fucking Chinaman!

Marta kept sobbing. He placed a hand on her head. My hand is trembling, like a schoolboy with his first bitch. Like it was trembling when I touched Gabriela in Yurécuaro. Or like that kid from the university I took that afternoon in Chapultepec. Or like those girl's hands trembled when I pulled down her panties. Even more when I snuck out from behind that tree. And that little bitch was a pretty thing, but she was as much a virgin as her fucking mother. Crying her eyes out but squeezing me so hard I could barely breathe. Fucking little brat! And now I'm trembling like that kid. The minute Marta's near me I start trembling. And she's just a hole with legs and she's not even pretending she's got her virginity to lose. Now, right now, is when I should make my move and drag her into bed. They say that women get hornier when they're crying. Fucking trembling hands!

He pulled away from Marta and motioned for her to sit down on the couch next to him. He lifted her chin and dried her tears with his handkerchief.

"Seems I'm always drying your tears, Marta."

"Yes."

"I don't have much experience at this, Marta."

"Me, neither, Filiberto. I thought I didn't know how to cry anymore."

She kissed him gently on his mouth, stood up, and went to the kitchen, taking the empty cup with her. García sat paralyzed, his eyes half closed, his lips pressed together so they wouldn't tremble. She beat me to it. Here's me with my mister-nice-guy routine, and she's the one who takes the bull by the horns. And right next to the window, so those fucking Russians could see everything. Or maybe she was sending them some kind of signal? But, a signal for what?

He stood up and went over to the window. He scanned the façade of the hotel across the street for the room they were spying from, but he couldn't see anything.

"Here's some more coffee, Filiberto. Do you want more cognac?"

"Thank you, but I've had enough."

"Sit and drink your coffee. You must be very tired ..."

"Marta, my dear ... You shouldn't do those things. Don't think I'm so old I don't feel ..."

Marta laughed.

"I'd be very upset if you didn't feel anything. I've just told you I'm not a child and ... and ever since the first day you walked into the shop ... Remember what you said to me? 'Can I write you a letter, my lovely?'"

"'Only if you write it in Chinese, Mr. Filiberto.'"

"You remember! You remember! From that day on I've been thinking about you ... imagining, fantasizing ..."

"Fantasizing what, Marta?"

"... and asking questions. And that's when they told me that you were in the police and that ... that you were famous for having killed a lot of people ..."

There was a long pause.

"It's true, Marta."

"Like those two men last night, criminals who wanted to kill you just because you were doing your job."

"Things aren't that simple, Marta."

"Now I know I was right, that you are good and I love you and I am going to love you forever. I'm not asking you for anything, Filiberto, nothing at all. I know I don't have the right to ask you for anything ..."

"You can ask me for anything you like, Marta."

"You don't know what it's like to be afraid, to always be afraid. For as long as I can remember, I've been afraid. And when you're afraid, when everything is filled with fear, you can't love. You are very brave and you don't know what it's like, but it's horrible ... To always be afraid and alone ..."

"But, I do, Marta dear, I do know, we are all afraid sometimes and we are all alone."

"You've never been married?"

"Who would ever marry a man like me, Marta? With my ... profession?"

"Many women. You don't know how good you are, the good you do in the world. In these last few weeks, all I did was wait for you to come into Mr. Liu's store and talk to me. And yesterday ... yesterday I thought I couldn't go on living like that, drowning in all that fear and loneliness. Anything was better than that ...

better than being without you. And that's why I left while you were eating with Mr. Liu and waited for you in the street so I could tell you the truth. Was that bad of me?"

"It was good of you, Marta."

"I don't regret doing it, and I'm never going to regret doing it. For the first time, because you're here, I'm living without fear ... because you know the whole truth ... because you can do whatever you want with me and I'll accept you ..."

"Marta, I ... also ... I want to tell you—"

The telephone rang.

"García?"

"Speaking."

"The person we talked to yesterday wants to see you as soon as possible."

"But—"

"We're sending a car from the office to pick you up. Wait outside."

"But, Colonel, it's just that—"

"Outside."

He hung up.

"You have to go out?"

"Yes."

"But that's not right. You're so tired, you barely slept last night, I heard you leaving at six this morning ..."

"I went to the Turkish baths. Goodbye, Marta."

"Should I make dinner for you?"

"I don't know when I'll be back, Marta. Go to sleep in the bedroom and—"

"I'll wait for you in the living room."

"I don't know when I'll be home. Go to bed and we'll talk tomorrow."

He went into the bedroom, picked up his hat, and returned to the living room. Marta hugged him and kissed him on the mouth. This kiss lasted a long time. She's leading the charge. And me acting like a chump, so paternal that she had to be the one to start things rolling. More like a faggot. Oh, dear, don't say such things, you'll make me blush! Faggot, fucking faggot! She's made me bashful. And those Russians, seeing and hearing everything, me being all fatherly and she wanting to get it on. And that fucking del Valle! Just when I'm making headway. And I've never done it with a Chinese gal! And she makes my head spin, it's not like with the others. Maybe all Chinese gals are like this. Or maybe I'm just out of my league. The gringo, the Russian ... and Marta! They're all in a different league—so professional, so Outer Mongolia, so international intrigue. And me, I'm just a stiff factory—assembly line. And Marta. Damn it! Even people wearing huaraches are digging their high heels into me. And I can't even make a play. Like I don't understand anything anymore. Like everything has to be explained to me very *very* slowly. Get with it, you foolish old man, you won't get anywhere with words! Then again, all those loving words from Marta make me smell a rat. Fucking Marta! She makes me do the stupidest things ...

Mr. del Valle's face beamed with goodness. García recounted, in a duly abridged version, what had happened the night before and about the fifty-dollar bills. Del Valle was deep in thought.

"This, Mr. García, does seem to indicate that there is some truth in the rumors."

"I think so, too, Mr. del Valle," the colonel said.

"But the evidence is only circumstantial, Colonel, only circumstantial, and, in a case as serious as this one, we must have proof. We have only one day left."

"We're doing everything humanly possible, Mr. del Valle. Besides García's investigation, we have doubled our surveillance on the borders, in hotels."

"The lives of two presidents are at stake, Colonel. I think we should arrest that Wang."

García spoke:

"I think it's better to leave him be and watch him. I don't think he's the one in charge, but he could lead us to the person who is."

"Your opinion, Colonel?"

"García's right. He's already being watched, around the clock, without his knowledge."

Del Valle turned back to García. That perfect political smile had returned to his lips.

"Congratulations, Mr. García. Needless to say, I deeply regret that you were put in a position where your life was in danger and you had to kill those two men. Killing is so repulsive."

"It was necessary, Mr. del Valle," the colonel said.

"Yes, yes, I understand. I'm not blaming anyone, I'm simply not used to this sort of thing, but to return to what I was saying before, I would like to congratulate you, Mr. García. In less than twenty-four hours you have given us enough information to confirm our suspicions. Excellent work, excellent."

García remained silent. His hat was on his lap, his eyes staring at nothing in particular.

"As a result of your brilliant investigation, Mr. García, we can positively confirm that money from Communist China is being used to to carry out an assassination attempt in Mexico."

"It appears that way, Mr. del Valle," said the colonel.

"Such a large amount of money, as well as the immediate measures they took as soon as they found out Mr. García was conducting an investigation, show us that we are dealing with a serious threat. The very fact that they tried to kill Mr. García, a Mexican policeman, is proof, in my mind, that our suspicions have been confirmed, without a shadow of a doubt."

There was silence. The colonel was playing with his gold lighter. García kept staring at nothing. Damn! If we're going to drum up international conspiracies every time somebody in Mexico wants to kill a cop, we're really fucked. How about one for every time some thug wants to hurry me on my way... Damn right I smell a rat.

Mr. del Valle continued:

"Gentlemen, I think we can take as a certainty that there is a conspiracy, originating in Communist China, to assassinate the president of the United States of America during his visit to our country."

He looked at both of them to watch the effect of his words. The colonel kept playing with his lighter. García kept looking at nothing.

"I don't need to add, gentlemen, that this conspiracy not only threatens the life of the president of the United States, but also our president, and world peace."

He paused again. The colonel was still entertaining himself with his lighter, García with nothingness.

"What is your opinion, Colonel?"

"You have analyzed the situation correctly, Mr. del Valle."

"I believe so. And you, Mr. García?"

"Maybe."

Del Valle, who had his congratulatory speech all prepared, was taken off guard. He was about to say something to García, but instead turned back to the colonel.

"We must triple our precautions. Mr. President will not like being forced to ride in an armored car, but let's not forget that such a vehicle should have been used in Dallas."

"I understand, Mr. del Valle."

"And even if we do resort to armored vehicles, which will be necessary if we fail to dismantle this conspiracy before the day after tomorrow, there remain several moments of serious danger. I'm thinking particularly of the unveiling of the statue in the park. Needless to say, we have searched all the surrounding buildings and have ordered security forces on all the balconies, but there is still danger ..."

"That's true, Mr. del Valle," the colonel said.

His eyes were half closed, staring at the lighter twirling in his fingers. Mr. del Valle turned to García with a grave expression on his face:

"In the meantime, Mr. García, you can see the importance, for all of us, for all Mexicans, of finding those Communist Chinese agents and liquidating them as soon as possible. Do I make myself clear?"

"Yes."

"I think the steps you've already taken are very important. What other measures are planned?"

"Tonight, in a few minutes, I'm going to meet the Russian and the gringo at Café Canton."

"Do you think that's a good idea?"

"No. But it's necessary. If these ... these Chinamen are planning something, we have to draw them out."

Del Valle stood up. Now this guy is going to deliver a speech about our nation and our loyalty to its institutions. Fucking loyalty!

"Mr. García, the matter is in your hands and, if you will allow me to say so, I admire your courage. I'm sure I don't need to tell you that you are putting your own life in danger."

"It's necessary, Mr. del Valle," the colonel said.

García stood up:

"I have to go."

"I understand, I understand," Mr. Del Valle said. "But before you leave here, Mr. García, I have to again express my admiration for your courage. These people, it seems, are quite serious, as the lamentable events of last night demonstrate."

"We're serious, too," the colonel said, standing up.

Mr. del Valle walked up to García:

"Mr. García, allow me to shake your hand. Our nation is proud of you. Your heroism, because that's what it is, heroism, must remain a secret, but the nation and our president will find a way to show their gratitude. I wish you the very best of luck."

"Thanks. Anything else, Colonel?"

"No. Good luck, García."

García walked out, but he could overhear Mr. del Valle's next comment:

"A crude man, like the great Centaurs of the North who made the Revolution ..."

Fucking Mr. Del Valle! Him and his independence day speeches. His mother is crude, the motherfucker. I'm just a professional gunslinger, a hit man on the payroll of the police. Why so many damn words? And if he wants me to whack those Chinamen, why doesn't he just come out and say so. Fucking Chinamen! Anyway, I've got it in for Liu—the sonofabitch beat me to it. Yeah, me and Pancho Villa, the Centaurs of the North. Hey, I'm from Yurécuaro, Michoacán, son of La Charanda and father unknown. And if they don't like it, they can all—absolutely all of them—go fuck their mothers. Fucking Charanda! And Marta there in my house, looking at me with my stupid mug. Her with all her kisses and hugs and me with my stupid mug. Maybe if instead of learning how to kill I'd learned how to give speeches, then I'd be like Rosendo del Valle. A dandy-ass. Or I'd end up like the professor, mooching booze for a living. And now our nation will be grateful. And what should I be grateful to our nation for? As my fellow countryman from Michoacán famously wrote: "If as a kid I went to school / and was a soldier when I grew / if as a husband she gave me horns / and then I died as was my due / What do I owe the sun / for having warmed my bones?"

Neither Graves nor Laski was in Café Canton. Wang was working the cash register and four young Chinamen were standing behind the counter. Only one of them lifted his eyes to look at García; his face revealed no surprise. He simply edged over toward the cash register, as if he was just doing his job, spoke quickly to old man Wang, then disappeared into what seemed to be the kitchen. García sat down in one of the booths and ordered a beer. These fucking Chinamen are getting nervous. Seems a good idea to come here, just to see what they'll do. Maybe even that restless soul from Sayula will show up. Fucking Mr. del Valle! "Killing is so repulsive." But when he was governor of his state, he brought with him everybody under his wing. He had General Miraflores with him as his chief of operations. Next thing it'll be Miraflores going on about how repulsive it is to kill. They've all become so damn upstanding. The Revolution turned government. Fuck the Revolution and fuck the fucking government!

Laski appeared at the door. I almost didn't see him coming. This fucking Russian seems to blend into other people and things. And now his eyes look even sadder than they did before.

"Is Graves coming?"

"Yeah."

"I'm going to order a glass of milk."

"Don't they have milk in your country?"

"Of course they do. In Russia we have everything, absolutely everything."

"There's only one Russia."

"Naturally, Russia is …"

"I was pulling your leg, Laski, my friend. What news have you got for me? Any new rumors from Outer Mongolia?"

"Ha, ha, ha … You are formidable, Filiberto, truly formidable."

"I'm going to make a call before Graves gets here. Excuse me."

He got up and walked over to the telephone. Wang didn't look up, but one of the young Chinamen was keeping a close eye on him, and the one who'd disappeared still hadn't returned.

They answered at La Ópera cantina, and in a few moments he was talking to the professor:

"What happened?"

"Everything went south, Cap'n. The gringa threw me out, she didn't even let me finish the bottle of rum. She said she was having a party with you and that everything was going to work out. So, what about my three hundred pesos?"

"Two hundred and fifty."

"So, what about it?"

"Tomorrow."

"The gringa is sure you're going there tonight, Cap'n."

"I just might."

"She's pretty washed up."

"See you tomorrow."

He hung up and returned to the table. Graves was already there, sitting across from the Russian. García sat down next to Graves.

"You two already met?"

"Yes," said Graves, "many years ago."

"Unfortunately," Laski said, "one cannot say that in all this time a true friendship has flourished between us."

Graves flashed his tourist smile:

"Ivan Mikhailovich tried to kill me in Constantinople in '57."

Ivan Mikhailovich's eyes grew even sadder still:

"A poorly planned job, very poorly planned. There was no time to make it foolproof."

The memory of his failure seemed to pain him deeply. Graves interrupted his sad reflections:

"I haven't been able to get the numbers of the bills. The Hong Kong Bank and, it seems, even the colony's English authorities have been unwilling to cooperate."

The Russian smiled. He seemed gratified.

"Allies and friends are not as friendly as they might seem," he said.

Graves paid no attention to the comment.

"However, we are certain that the transaction was carried out. One of our agents in Kowloon confirms it."

"Did you doubt my informants, Graves, my friend?"

"Yes, Ivan Mikhailovich. When the KGB gives us a present, we study it very carefully before accepting it ..."

"Don't look a gift horse in the mouth," the Russian said.

"The Trojans sure should have," said Graves. "The transaction was carried out nine days ago. The money was requested in fifty-dollar bills, American dollars, and was picked up by several men, some Chinese, some Western. If we insist, and we are going to insist, we can get the numbers, but not for a couple of weeks, at least ..."

"When it will already be too late," García said.

"Too late indeed. But everything must be known. Even if only to understand the extent of the conspiracy and round up all those involved."

"There are too many people involved for a job like this," García said.

"When the Chinese do something, they do it on a grand scale," the Russian said. "Over there, everything is grand."

"But there are too many," García insisted. "You only need two or three to plan an attack like this, at most."

"I've been thinking the same thing," Graves said.

Laski was slowly sipping his milk. Graves, after his experience with the coffee, was drinking a beer, as was García.

"For instance, it seems that all the Chinamen in this restaurant are involved," García said. "It doesn't make sense that waiters could organize an attack of that magnitude."

"Maybe we're up a blind alley, Ivan Mikhailovich, my friend."

"I don't know, Graves. We are investigating, that is all. You should have learned by now that in our profession investigations are conducted in order to reach an unknown truth. What that truth is doesn't matter to us and, if we knew it beforehand, there'd be no reason to investigate."

"Only execute," García said.

"Precisely, Filiberto, only execute. But now our task is only to investigate, because the moment to execute has not yet arrived."

The fourth Chinaman returned from the kitchen to his place behind the counter. He exchanged a few words with Wang, then went back to his work. Not once did he look at the three men sitting in the booth.

"Oh, and Filiberto," Laski suddenly said, "I have of course given orders to stop surveillance on you, and on you, too, Graves, my friend."

"I did, too," Graves said. "What Mr. García said is absolutely true. This was starting to look like a child's game. That's what I told my bosses. I told them that you, García, had pointed out our mistake. They were very impressed."

"Thanks."

"What are we going to do tonight?" Laski asked. "If it's just a matter of getting together socially …"

"The Chinese are worried, Ivan Mikhailovich."

"They sure are," Graves said. "It's almost impossible to investigate anyone without them noticing. This afternoon in the warehouses there was a lot of activity. I'd like to investigate ..."

"They might do us the favor," said García. "That's why we're here, just to see what these fellows do."

"They could be planning to kill us," Laski said. "I've never liked to be the bait in the trap."

"Me, neither. But that's what we are now, Ivan Mikhailovich."

"I agree with García. The best thing is to provoke them to make a move; there's no time for anything else."

One of the Chinese men came out from behind the counter and over to the table. He was young and strong, with an expressionless face.

"Can I get you anything else?"

García looked up and stared at him. The Chinamen didn't look away.

"We're talking," García said, in a harsh voice.

The Chinaman shrugged his shoulders, walked over to the door, and leaned against it without taking his eyes off them. *This Chinaman is looking for a thrashing, even actively requesting one. Maybe they want us out of here. They must want us out of here, but they can go to hell. And this gringo doesn't stop smiling like a moron. And the Russian looks like he's about to cry. Fucking Outer Mongolia! We've got to give these fucking Chinamen one more chance.*

"I'm going to the men's room," he said, standing up.

He walked to the back of the restaurant, entered the restroom, and walked over to the urinal. *Now's the time, if they're serious, they'll come looking for me here and then we'll see whose hide yields more whips, as they say. Just a matter of giving them time. Anyway, time is what there's lots of in this fucking* life. And Marta fast asleep in my bed and me here acting like a chump. Now they'll be able to say they caught me with my pants down.

He heard the door open and people entering. He didn't turn around to see who they were. Let them keep coming, very quietly, like ducks in a pond. As long as they don't stick a knife in my back. Fucking knifes. Let them think they've got the upper hand . . .

A voice said something quickly in Chinese. García turned, .45 in hand. There was a man on either side. One hit his wrist with an open chop and the gun fell to the floor. The other jumped him put him in a choke hold. At that moment, when he thought he was done for, the door swung open. It was Graves, without his glasses, entering like a whirlwind. He took one huge leap, and his feet landed on the back of the man squeezing García's throat. The other man fell on him but a blow to his forehead forced him back, dazed. García, now free, finished him off with a punch in the face that smashed his nose. In the meantime, Graves had the other in a chokehold and had forced him onto his knees, his eyes popping out of his head and his face dripping sweat. Graves gave him a chop on his neck, right on his Adam's apple. The man let out a muffled groan and collapsed onto the floor, his head falling into the urinal. The other, blood pouring out of his nose, opened the door and ran out. García picked up his gun and put it back in its holster after checking to make sure there was no damage. Graves was smiling, as always, as he put on his glasses.

"I figured why you came here, García, and I had your back."

"Thanks."

"You were right. We've scared these Chinamen, and that's revealing."

"Right."

"Laski stayed at the table so the others wouldn't become alarmed. They must think they've taken us prisoner or whatever they wanted to do. Now what?"

"Now we go out and pretend nothing happened, then we leave. We delivered our message. I'll tell the police to keep an eye on this place."

Standing in front of the dirty, broken mirror, he slicked down his hair that had gotten mussed and straightened out the handkerchief in the chest pocket of his jacket. The Chinaman on the floor began to show signs of life.

"What do we do with this one, García?"

"Leave him, Graves. He's an underling, he doesn't matter."

Satisfied with his grooming, he walked out, followed by Graves. They acted like they were simply leaving the bathroom. The Chinamen behind the counter were surprised to see them. Wang lifted his eyes and for a split second looked petrified. Laski was still at the table, pretending not to be aware of anything, but his hand was inside his jacket, on the butt of his gun. García walked straight to the register:

"Our check."

Wang looked at García with panic in his eyes. He did some quick calculations on an abacus and said:

"Seven pesos."

"Here. Give the other three to the fellow who cleans the bathroom so he'll do a better job next time. It's dirty in there."

Laski and Graves had joined him, Laski carrying his hat. García took it from him and put it on.

"Thanks," he said.

They walked outside.

"My car is across the street," Graves said.

They crossed the street and got into the car, a dark-colored Buick. All three sat in the front seat.

"Let's go to Guerrero Street," García said. "You know where it is?"

"Yeah. What's there?"

"We're going to pay a visit to one of your compatriots, Graves. The widow of Roque Villegas Vargas. Maybe being a fellow American and all, she'll tell you more."

He told them about Anabella.

"Maybe you can get the truth out of her if you threaten to take away her American passport."

"Let's go."

"But first I have to make a phone call."

"I have a radio in the car you can use …"

"I prefer a public phone, no offense. Stop there, at the tobacconist."

"I'll make sure we're not being followed," Laski said. "As you said, it's ill advised to be the bait in a trap …"

His eyes had become as sad as his voice. García got out of the car and asked for the telephone.

"García here, Colonel."

"What do you want? You left less than an hour ago …"

"I was with my friends at Café Canton."

"Good for you!"

The colonel's voice had that mocking tone of superiority it got sometimes.

"We had an altercation …"

"Were you drunk?"

"No, Colonel. But they don't want us there. And it seems there's been a lot of movement at the warehouses in Nonoalco, where Wang has his merchandise. Maybe the dough is there …"

"I'll look into it."

The colonel hung up. Damn! I mention that dough and he doesn't even have time to say goodbye. He's probably already left like a bat out of hell. And me playing the chump. I should've left them with their international intrigue and gone after the dough. Fucking international intrigue! Five hundred thousand bucks. That's a very tidy sum. And me stuck in Outer Mongolia. Fucking Outer Mongolia!

He got in the car.

"Nobody's following us," Laski said. "I think Graves told the truth for a change, and he doesn't have men on our tail."

"I always tell the truth," Graves said. "At least when it's convenient. And such moments do turn up now and then."

"Not often," the Russian said, "not often."

"Are they going to watch the warehouses?" Graves asked. "That's important."

"Yeah. Let's get going."

García knocked on the door of apartment number 9. Nobody answered.

"The bird's probably already flown," Laski said.

"Don't think so," García said. "She was too eager to collect the money and the car. Who wants to open the door?"

"It's a cinch," Graves said, "but I would like to observe the method used by my Soviet colleague. Someone told me that for him there is no such thing as an impenetrable lock or safe."

Laski smiled, pleased, and leaned over the door handle.

"Very common. But I think we are being remiss in our manners. We should leave this job to our friend, Filiberto, our host."

"Just do it, Ivan Mikhailovich ..."

"No, it would be rude. At international conferences, and this is an international conference, the representative of the host country always presides. It's all yours, Filiberto."

García took hold of the handle and turned. The door opened.

"They didn't lock it," Graves said.

They entered and García turned on the light. The room was still a mess. Only one thing was different. The corpse of what had once been Anabella Ninziffer, of Wichita Falls, alias Anabella Crawford, was sprawled out on the sofa. Someone had strangled her with an electrical cord. Laski went up and felt her wrist.

"Not long ago. Two hours at the most ..."

"Whoever killed her," said García, "left the door open, because they planned to return."

"Why return?" Graves asked. "They killed her so she wouldn't talk, that's all."

"But they must have also thought it wouldn't be a good idea to leave a corpse in plain sight, that it'd be better to hide it. Then the police would think she'd split."

He entered the bedroom. All of Anabella's clothes had been thrown haphazardly into a suitcase on the bed.

"Maybe she was thinking of running away," Graves said.

"She wouldn't have packed her clothes like that," said Laski, who stood in the doorway looking in. "Women, especially performers, take good care of their clothes."

"They must've planned to take it all away," García said.

They went back to the living room. Graves ran his eyes over everything.

"What should we do? Shouldn't we notify the police?"

"Better to wait for her killers. Do you agree, Ivan Mikhailovich?" García asked.

"We have to turn off the light and close the door, just as they left it."

García closed the door and turned off the light. Some light from the street and a flashing red neon sign entered the room through the open window. Every time it flashed on, the neon lit up Anabella's open eyes. They sat at the dining table, near the window, where they could watch the street.

"She'd look drunk if her eyes were closed," Laski said. "I've never liked drunk women."

"She probably was drunk," García said. "Maybe she didn't even realize what was about to happen. Doesn't seem like she put up much of a struggle."

"It's not easy to strangle someone without a struggle," Graves said.

"An electrical cord is very effective. Don't you think so, Filiberto?"

García was going to say that he'd never used one, but then he remembered the one time he had. It was in Huasteca, and I was carrying out orders. Puny old devil who spent the whole day in his rocking chair on the porch of his house. The Boss gave the order. I came up behind him with the cord. They told me to make sure there was no fuss, so I waited till it was getting dark, around seven at night. When he stopped moving, I put him in a coffin we had brought, and we took the main road out of town. The best way to carry a body discreetly is in a coffin. A laborer coming down the road with his oxen even doffed his hat when he saw it. Then, suddenly, as we turned a corner, the fucking old man started kicking. Like he wanted someone to notice. We had to lower the coffin, open it, and give him another squeeze with the same cord. Fucking rowdy old man! His name was Remigio Luna.

Graves said:

"Not everyone puts up a fight. In Vienna, four years ago, I

found it necessary to liquidate an agent. I think he was a colleague of yours, Ivan Mikhailovich. I gave one strong pull. First I wrapped my hands in handkerchiefs to protect them. He didn't budge. He just made a gurgling sound."

"That was Dimitrios Mikropopulos," Laski said. "A very effective man, sometimes, but of unstable temperament and rather inclined to be disloyal, like all Levantines."

"That was him," Graves said. "A double agent . . ."

He got up and covered Anabella's face with a newspaper that was lying on the floor. Now, the neon lit with reddish tones the photograph of Roque Villegas, already dead, printed on the front page of the newspaper.

"A few years ago," Laski suddenly said, "a Chinese colleague . . ."

"When the Russians were their friends," Graves clarified.

"Yes. He always carried a thin silk cord in his bag. He claimed it was the most efficient method. Once I asked him why he didn't use nylon, and he told me that nylon stretches a little under pressure and is not as effective as silk. I think his preference was simply Chinese reactionaryism."

"That was Sing Po!" Graves exclaimed. "I never did find out what happened to him. I met him once in Seoul, but then he disappeared . . ."

"The silk cord, as it turned out, was not such a sure thing after all. He wanted to use it one too many times, when he shouldn't have. I stabbed him in the stomach. That was in Constantinople . . ."

"You don't say . . ." Graves said.

They sat in silence: men who knew how to wait.

"I heard you always use a .45, García."

"I used to use a 32-20, but the bullets are narrow and not

immediately effective. Once, a guy with three bullets in him almost stabbed me."

"I prefer German Lugers," Laski said.

"We mostly use revolvers," Graves said. "They have only six shots, but they're reliable. It's rare you have a chance to use all of them, anyway. Usually one's enough."

"Lugers, just like American pistols," Laski said, "have to be kept very clean. But if they're well cared for, they're very effective. For a while, in Canada, I had to use an American .45, Graves, and I must confess, it served me very well."

"Thanks," Graves said. "I once had the chance to use a Russian submachine gun, and I can assure you, that is a terrific weapon."

They sat in silence again. Anabella Ninziffer was showing too much leg. Fucking gringa! Seems we're holding a wake. And what, exactly, did the dead woman die of? Well, she caught a fever. Oh, yeah, a fever my ass! Your dead woman barely had a sniffle, but she died anyway. With a light cord wrapped around her neck. And with bare legs. These gringas are indecent even when they're dead. And we were going to have a *party*. A wake, for this old bitch! Half a million dollars just to kill this bag of rags. These Chinamen are real morons.

"García, my friend," Graves said, "do you think there's any rum left?"

"Maybe, in the kitchen."

"Hopefully there's milk in the refrigerator," Laski said. "Americans always have milk. They are big milk drinkers."

García stood up. No matter what, since we're in Mexico, it seems I have to play the host. Fucking host. Please, welcome to my humble abode, make yourself at home with the fucking stiff.

He found a bottle of rum on the counter in the kitchen,

and several bottles of beer in the refrigerator, but no milk. He brought the rum and two beers into the dining room.

"No milk."

"That's the problem with civilizing these Americans," Laski said. "Before, they always had milk in their homes, but then, during the two wars, they learned about drinking, and now they don't drink milk anymore. We have lost a lot by civilizing them. Hand me a beer, Filiberto."

Graves picked up the bottle of rum and took a slug, while García and Laski enjoyed their beers. They continued to wait. That was their job, to wait, so that when the time came, they could kill with a sure hand. Anabella Ninziffer's legs shone white in the darkness. García got up and covered them with another piece of newspaper. Fucking gringa! And Graves drinks and drinks and never gets drunk. I bet he's never been drunk in his life. And he's good at karate. I should have learned that as a kid, but there were other things to learn, like how to stay alive.

They continued to wait.

"Mexican rum is very good," Graves said suddenly.

"Thanks," García said. "Do you want another beer, Ivan Mikhailovich?"

"Yes, please. And, please forgive me for not going myself, but I prefer not to turn my back on either of you in the dark."

García went to get two more beers. Fucking suspicious Russian! What are these two thinking about? Their own faithful departed? They don't have a conscience. Gringo and Russian. Not a conscience between them. At least the gringo covered up the dead woman's eyes. Maybe she reminds him of someone he shacked up with. Fucking gringo! All that shit about Vienna and Constantinople! They must see what a chump I am.

"Here's your beer, Ivan Mikhailovich."

"Thanks, Filiberto. It's going to be very bad for me ..."

García sat down. His hand felt for his .45 that he'd left on the seat next to him. Got to stay alert in the dark. Especially with these two.

"Not that we don't trust you, Filiberto, but I don't like you having your hand on your gun."

"The darkness," Graves said, "breeds bad thoughts."

They continued to wait. Nobody has said, like at wakes, how good and kind the dead woman was. For all I know they'll say that at my wake. Marta says so. And she's lying in my bed and I'm here pretending to be a big shot in international intrigue. Along with these two guys who know more tricks than an old fox. And what's this crap about darkness breeding bad thoughts? Do either of them ever have any good thoughts? Touch your forehead first, so God will free you from bad thoughts. That's what I was taught to say in Yurécuaro. These fellows should touch their foreheads first. But as far as I can tell, they don't even cross themselves. And those who don't know God will kneel before any old sonofabitch, let alone the devil. Forehead first, also with the bullet, so they don't budge. Like that guy in Tabasco. He jumped around like a decapitated lizard. Forehead first, like a true Christian. It'd be good to pray for the dead woman, but I don't remember any of the prayers they say at wakes. It's strange that I never go to wakes. Maybe it's because it takes one person to make the dead and another to pray for them.

Laski suddenly spoke, quietly, as someone does in the presence of a corpse.

"Might seem strange, but sometimes I do think about death."

Graves laughed.

"It's just that one day it'll be our turn," Laski continued. "We get used to seeing it come to others, but we must remember that one day it will come to us."

"He who lives by the sword, dies by the sword," Graves said. "That's in the Bible."

"Yes," said Laski. "We also study the Bible in Russia. It is an interesting book. And our great writers have dealt often with the problem of death."

"And your great leaders have employed it," said Graves.

"One cannot govern without killing, Graves, my friend. All governments have learned this by now. That's why *we* exist."

"To conduct investigations," Graves said, curtly.

"And to kill when the time comes to kill," Laski insisted again, his voice low. "Yes, to kill. But I wasn't thinking about that. I was thinking about the death that will come to each one of us. We kill, but we don't know what it is to die. As if we said, we are death's doormen, but we always remain outside."

"You Russians, you'd rather be dead than feel left out."

"Welcome to your death, we tell people. But we remain outside, until the day comes for us to enter. As if we were in the dentist's waiting room. And deep down, we feel certain that our turn will never come, even though we know it will."

"Are you afraid to die?" Graves asked, curious.

"Only those who know nothing of death are not afraid. We know too much."

They continued to wait. These guys are turning philosophical on me. Every dog has his day. And there's a bullet out there with each of our names on it. Or an electric cord, like this fucking gringa. Or maybe even pneumonia. He died in his bed, with last rites and a blessing from the pope. Damn! I've never thought of that. The colonel will die in his bed, same with Rosendo del Valle. There are categories of deaths, and there are men who are in the category of dying in their bed, with last rites. Straight to heaven. And when you get there, you turn into an angel. For all I know, this gringa already has her wings and her halo. Though she didn't die in bed. And she of all people should have died in bed because when she was alive, that's what she used most. But she had the bum luck to get involved in this international intrigue. And there's Marta in my bed. So lovely, and all alone in my bed. And this gringa who wanted to leave her slutty life behind and enter the life of international intrigue. And they did her in with an electrical cord, and she couldn't even make it back to bed, which is all she ever knew. And by the time she realized it, she was having a wake instead of a party. Fucking gringa!

They continued to wait.

At about four in the morning a car stopped in front of the building. The three men stood up. Graves cautiously looked out the window.

"Two men are getting out," he said. "There's a third in the car..."

Laski and García placed themselves on either side of the door to the apartment. But first, García removed the newspapers covering the dead woman. Graves remained at the dining table, in the dark. All three had their guns drawn.

A few minutes later the door opened and one man, then another, entered.

"Don't move," García said.

Laski turned on the light and slammed the door shut. Their two visitors were Chinese, one who they'd seen in Café Canton. They looked around slowly and saw the three cops, guns drawn. Their faces showed no emotion. Graves stepped forward and frisked them. One was carrying a gun and the other a knife.

"That's all," Graves said.

He placed the weapons on the dining table. The two men, their hands raised, had not moved. Graves said:

"We've got to bring in the guy in the car."

He left quickly. Laski said:

"Sit in those two chairs, against the wall."

One of the Chinamen said something in Cantonese. García smashed him across the mouth with the butt of his gun. His lip split open and blood gushed out.

"Shut up, and if you do speak, make sure it's in a Christian language."

"I understand Cantonese" Laski said.

"That's why it's better if we all speak Spanish. Sit down."

The two Chinamen sat down.

"He was telling his friend not to talk."

"Let him say it in Spanish. And you, too, Ivan Mikhailovich, if you've got something to say, say it in Spanish."

The Chinamen sat absolutely still in their chairs, like two ancient emperors on their thrones. Graves opened the door and entered, pushing ahead of him another Chinaman, his face covered in blood.

"He didn't want to come," he said.

They sat the third Chinaman down. Graves pointed at Anabella's corpse.

"Why did you kill her?"

"She is of no importance," said the Chinaman who had spoken Cantonese. His Spanish was perfect.

"Why did you kill her?" García asked in turn.

"She wanted money."

"Why?"

"She is of no importance."

"That's why you killed her?"

"How much money do you want? We can give you money, a lot of money. More than any Mexican policeman has ever seen in his life."

"How much money?"

"A thousand dollars, American dollars."

García slapped him across the face. The Chinaman almost fell off his chair. He got up and wiped off the blood that was dripping from his mouth.

"Five thousand dollars. Five thousand dollars, in cash, for each of you."

"In cash?"

"Yes."

"In fifty-dollar bills?"

"If you want."

"Where's the money?"

"Sounds like a good deal, doesn't it?"

"I want to see the money."

"We'll give it to you."

"Now."

"Okay."

"Come on."

"I have to go get it."

"Sonofabitch Chink. You think we're going to let you go?"

"I promise you, we have the money."

"Where?"

"We have it. One goes. Two stay here."

"Why don't you call someone and tell them to bring it?"

The Chinamen thought for a moment. This is the one who gives the orders, at least to these two others. He doesn't even consult them. And I think he's Cuban, the way he drops his *s*'s. Now things really are complicated, now that Cubans are mixed up in it.

The Chinaman said:

"I'll make a call."

"There it is, on the table, next to your girlfriend."

The Chinaman got up and walked over to the telephone. To reach it, he had to move one of Anabella's legs out of the way. He dialed the number. Laski stood next to him. All three watched him dial. 3-5-9-9-0-8. When someone picked up, the Chinaman spoke quickly in Cantonese. He did not beg. It sounded like he was giving orders. He hung up abruptly and returned to his chair.

"He'll be here in twenty minutes," he said.

"What did he say, Ivan Mikhailovich?"

"He spoke to someone named Feng. He told him to bring fifteen thousand dollars."

"Did he specifically say it should be in fifty-dollar bills?"

"No. And there was one part I didn't understand. Sounded like a code."

"I gave him the address of the house," the Chinaman said.

García turned to Graves.

"Tie them up, Graves. They say that you FBI agents take special classes in how to tie people up."

Graves went into the bedroom and returned with two sheets. He tore them into strips and quickly tied up the three Chinamen. Now they looked like half-wrapped mummies. Graves smiled as he reviewed his handiwork.

"It's easy," he said, "especially if you tie them to a chair. The position itself prevents them from struggling. And if they do, they fall over and are rendered completely helpless."

"Very interesting," Laski said, "but I think one of us should go out and watch for the new arrival. Just in case he decides to bring along some friends."

"He's coming alone," the Chinaman said.

Laski was holding his Luger like it was something that disgusted him.

"I think Mr. Graves should go."

"Why not you, Laski?" Graves asked. "I went last time."

"But I understand Cantonese and someone who understands Cantonese should stay here. The honor of watching the street is yours, Graves, my friend."

"I can watch from the window," Graves said.

He positioned himself where he could see the street without being seen from outside. Without taking his eyes off the street, he said:

"I'm interested in hearing the conversation here."

"Fine," said Laski. "Interrogate them, Filiberto."

Now that stinking rat's tail is starting to show. I sure as hell hope my two colleagues don't kick up a fuss about the money. Maybe they didn't even notice the number the Chinaman dialed. 3-5-9-9-0-8. That's where the dough must be, the ten thousand fifty-dollar bills. Fucking bills!

The Chinaman said:

"You aren't with the Mexican police."

"What job was Roque Villegas doing?"

The Chinaman was quiet.

"Look, Chink, no matter what, you're going to talk. You might as well make it easy on yourself."

"We're going to give you money."

"The money that came from Hong Kong?"

"Why do you care where it came from? It's good money."

"Did it come from Hong Kong?"

"Yes."

"Why did they send it to you?"

"For business."

"With that amount of money, you could open five hundred restaurants. Why did they send it?"

"Are you going to take the money Mr. Feng is bringing?"

"We've got to know where it came from. What business did they send the money for?"

"If you let us go, we'll give you more when this business is over."

"What business?"

The Chinaman was silent. García grabbed his earlobe and started twisting it. A few drops of blood oozed out.

"What business?"

"You already know. I know you. You're with the narcotics police ... And the other two are probably from across the border. It won't be the first time we arrange things with money, here and on the other side."

García let go of his ear. The Chinaman's face was still expressionless.

"Opium?"

"Morphine and heroine. We're buying it here to take to the States. Villegas was one of our contacts."

"How big?"

"Big. But Villegas told this woman everything and when you killed him last night, she wanted in, in exchange for keeping quiet."

"So you had her killed."

"That's how this sort of person is usually dealt with."

"True. And the money was sent to you from Hong Kong?"

"Yes."

Graves, next to the window, spoke:

"Why did they bring the money from Hong Kong? The Mafia has enough money ..."

"We aren't with the Mafia in the States. We're working against them," the Chinaman said.

"Your colleagues, have they got names?" Graves asked

"One of your poets asked: 'What's in a name? That which

we call a rose by any other name would smell as sweet.' Our colleagues, no matter what their names, would stink just as bad, Mr. Policeman."

Graves spoke without taking his eyes off the street:

"It's unusual to find a drug trafficker who quotes Shakespeare."

"Yes, Mr. Policeman. You people are used to dealing with coarse, uneducated men, men from the unions and the Mafia."

"The money comes from Peking?" Laski suddenly asked.

The Chinaman smiled, surprised:

"Yes, we've dropped several hints that this money might have come from Mr. Mao. It would be inconvenient if the authorities in Hong Kong and Macao were alerted, or the Mafia."

"All this money, it's for opium?" Graves asked.

"That money and a whole lot more. The opium business, and a lot of other ones."

"Like the assassination business," García threw out.

The Chinaman looked at him scornfully:

"That kind of business, Mr. García, can be carried out with local money and local talent. You should know that better than anybody."

The Chinaman smiled. Fucking Chink. Cheeky bastard. Trying to tell me that all this mess is just about drugs being moved across the border. Could be yes, could be no, the only sure thing is, we don't know. And we just keep investigating.

Graves said:

"I think Mr. García is talking about a different kind of assassination, one of greater magnitude, we could say."

"If you're talking about members of the Mafia, when they have to be dealt with, we arrange things in the States. It's not expensive to kill there."

"He was talking about something else," Graves said.

"You see, Mr. Policeman, we're going to take over the Mafia's entire business. And to do that, we need that money, and a whole lot more."

"My colleague here was talking about much more important targets than Mafia capos," Laski said. "Among your various projects, might there be one to assassinate the president of the United States?"

The Chinaman burst out laughing.

"What an odd notion. What would we gain from the death of the president of the United States? No, gentleman, no. We've always left that kind of business in the hands of the Americans. Or maybe you think we planned the attack in Dallas? No, no. Mr. García has worked before in cases of drug trafficking across the border."

"I'm from the FBI," Graves said. "Not from the Bureau of Narcotics. And this gentleman is from the Soviet secret service. As you can see, this is much more serious than you think."

The Chinaman sat in silence. He looked surprised.

"Now I understand," he said finally. "That's why we've been feeling so much pushback. Who told you that we were planning to assassinate the president?"

"You did," García said. "I'd just been given my assignment, and you sent someone to my house."

"I won't deny we hired Villegas to watch you, Mr. García. You came to Café Canton last night and were watching us. We know you've worked with drugs and the conclusion was obvious, and we thought it wise to watch you. Unfortunately, Villegas was clumsy, very clumsy And he has paid for it with his life. We had to employ local talent, quite inadequate, because there was nobody else available, and because, forgive me for saying so, Mr. García, we didn't consider you very important. It looked to us like a quite routine problem."

"Have your operations in the United States already begun?" Graves asked.

The Chinaman turned to look at him and smiled:

"Mr. Policeman, we are going to give you money so that you won't talk about this ever again, about this business that is so terribly unimportant compared to what you are investigating …." Suddenly, he became very serious, as if he had understood something. "But now I think that you are not going to accept our money, and that this is a trap. If you are investigating something so important …"

"Someone's coming. He's entered the building," Graves said.

García quickly gagged the Chinamen and stood next to the door, his gun in his hand. Laski stood on the other side. Graves hid behind the dining table. The three Chinamen remained sitting in front of the door. What am I going to do with the dough this Chink is bringing? Who knows what these fellows are up to, but they must like dough. Five thousand bucks wouldn't be bad. And then they can continue their investigations. And the bad part is that I think this guy is telling the truth, at least part of the truth. That was too much money for an assassination. Fucking Russians! Fucking Outer Mongolia!

The door swung open and a round of machine gun fire exploded into the room. It looked like the three Chinamen leapt up, chairs and all, then landed in a pile next to the window. Then the man entered, machine gun in hand, looking around. Graves, from the dining room, fired one shot. The man tottered, then fell to his knees as he was trying to lift the machine gun to fire again. García stepped forward and smashed him over the head with the butt of his gun. The man fell to the floor. García turned him over with his foot.

"He's not Chinese," he said.

"Let's get out of here," Graves said.

He took off running, followed by Laski and García. Pandemonium had broken out in the building: people shouted out to call the police, doors opened then slammed shut. García, Graves, and Laski ran down the stairs. One man tried to stop them, but when he saw them all with their guns drawn, he immediately backed off. They got to the street. Someone shot at them. They piled into Graves's car and sped off.

"We need a telephone," Graves said.

"At Sanborns," García said.

When they got there, they each went to a separate phone.

"Sorry for waking you, Colonel."

"You didn't. Someone else did a few minutes ago with a report of a shootout on Guerrero Street, 208, apartment 9."

"Yes, Colonel. There are five dead."

"I told you I wanted that woman alive."

"I didn't kill anybody."

"I wanted to talk to that woman."

"She was already dead when I arrived. And there's something else . . ."

"More dead?"

"No. Something important."

"What?"

"I think we're pissing outside the pot."

"What do you mean?"

"Those Chinamen are in a different business."

"What business?"

"Drugs. For the States."

"What, they have nothing to do with the other business?"

"I'm not so sure."

"Do you know or not?"

"Some things don't line up, Colonel."

"Like what?"

"Like, for example: who is Luciano Manrique, the guy who was stabbed?"

"Didn't you tell me he was Villegas's partner?"

"Maybe not, Colonel."

"By the look of it, you're only sure about the people you kill. Maybe that's why you like to kill them. I'm going to look at the file. Hold on."

"Yes, Colonel."

He held on. Fucking colonel! Telling me I'm only sure of the ones I kill. And him there all nice and cozy in his house, sleeping in his silk pajamas. And Marta sleeping in my bed and me here acting like a chump. And they killed that Chinaman right under my nose. And Marta? And who's keeping the Chinamen informed? Fucking Chinamen!

"García."

"Yes, Colonel."

"Call me in fifteen minutes. The gentleman we've been dealing with wants to be briefed."

"Okay."

The colonel hung up. It was almost five in the morning and there were very few people in the restaurant. Laski was sitting alone, drinking a glass of milk. He didn't do much reporting. Maybe he doesn't have to report to anybody. And me with the colonel and that fucking del Valle.

He walked over to Laski's table:

"Our colleague Graves had to go write up a report, or something like that."

García realized that he was hungry. He hadn't eaten anything since noon.

"You want to have something to eat?"

"No, just my glass of milk. That beer upset my stomach."

García ordered a steak and fries and sat down.

"Now, Ivan Mikhailovich, what do you say about your conspiracy?"

"I don't know. From the beginning, we said they were only rumors."

"The police are searching Wang's warehouses and Café Canton. If they find a large quantity of drugs, that'll settle it."

"We can't be sure of anything," Laski repeated.

"Even so, it's damn strange that a rumor would have reached Outer Mongolia about a gang of drug traffickers on the Mexican border. Don't you think?"

"I do. In any case, my government believed that the rumors were persistent enough to alert your government."

"And the Americans?"

"It was their president, or so it seemed, who was in danger."

"Do they produce opium in Outer Mongolia?"

"Not as far as I know. It's mostly desert. And very cold."

"How do you think the rumor got out there?"

"I don't know. Rumors get around."

"The one with the machine gun wasn't Chinese. I think he was Cuban."

"Really?"

"Yeah, Cuban. Those two-toned shoes, only Cubans wear those anymore."

They brought his dish. Laski sipped his milk in silence and with a certain amount of peevishness. García cut into his steak. It was too raw. I don't like to cut my meat and have blood squirt out. I'm not a lion. Fucking meat!

He called over the waiter and asked him to cook it longer. Then he excused himself from Laski and returned to the telephone.

"Colonel, García here."

"The gentleman you know wants to see you, in two hours. At seven."

"That's fine. By the way, one of the dead men was Cuban, wasn't he?"

"We have been able to identify only one of the Chinese. He was a Cuban citizen."

"And the one with the machine gun?"

"We still don't know who he was. By the way, I'd like, once in a while, for you to leave someone alive, someone we can question."

"I'll do my best, Colonel."

When he returned to the table, his steak was there and well cooked. Laski was eating a piece of chocolate cake. García sat down.

"In Mexico we have a saying when you get somebody else to do your dirty work, we say your using a cat's paw to pull your chestnuts out of the fire."

"Yes, Filiberto, many countries have similar expressions. Also in the Soviet Union ..."

Laski's large eyes exhibited nothing but total innocence.

"What were you saying?"

"I think it's fine to get the FBI to work for you, but I don't like it that you get me to work for you, especially when I'm just starting something up with that gal."

"She is very pretty, Filiberto. Looks like you have things all sewn up. Just this afternoon she kissed you on the mouth."

"I thought you'd stopped watching me."

"I have many men working for me. I must keep them busy doing something. Don't you agree?"

"Why don't you have them watching the Cubans?"

García's voice was sharp. Laski stopped smiling. He looked concerned:

"You are upset that we saw you with the girl, Filiberto. But it doesn't matter. We are all men and we all know how these things are."

"I don't like that kind of joke."

"I'm sorry, Filiberto, but it's all part of the game. When you get involved in these international affairs, nothing is private. I'm sorry, but that's the way it is." Laski's voice had also gotten hard.

"I have a theory, Ivan Mikhailovich."

"After a violent incident, I get hungry. It is interesting to observe the different ways men react. We have studied the reactions of each enemy agent, and we keep files on them all. Graves, for example, after every violent incident, feels an uncontrollable urge to report to his superiors. Perhaps it is due to a primitive need to confess a sin, or a longing—a very American longing, needless to say—to make every act legal."

"I was about to tell you my theory, Ivan Mikhailovich."

"On the same subject? It must be very interesting. Perhaps you've observed things we haven't. The truth is, the perfect agent should have no reaction at all to violence and death—emotional reactions are completely useless, though difficult to avoid. For instance, I get hungry, and then, when I eat, I get a stomachache. I have thought it's an inherited characteristic, perhaps a throwback to when man killed only to eat. What do you think?"

"Back to the chestnuts and the fire and the cat," García said. "We could formulate a theory about how you Russians, there in Outer Mongolia, heard certain rumors—"

"As we always said, they are only rumors. But Mexico has friendly diplomatic relations with the Soviet Union, and we believed it would be a noble act on our part to inform you of these rumors—you don't have any agents in Outer Mongolia."

"No, we don't."

The Russian's eyes filled with innocence and love for his fellow man.

"But you can count on us, Filiberto. Any rumor that might affect your country, we are more than willing to report it to you."

"Like this one?"

"Yes, like this one. It is a manifestation of the Soviet Union's sincerity and—"

"You know something, Ivan Mikhailovich? I think your reaction to violence is not to eat, but to talk, and above all, not to let anybody else talk."

"You think so? How interesting—"

"Now, to return to my theory—"

"Your reaction, Filiberto, is curious. I don't think I've ever seen a case like yours. You form theories, so many theories. And if you have nothing better to do, I think it would be a good time to go get some sleep."

"You might be right. We're wasting our time."

He paid and left. They said goodbye to each other at the door after making a date for twelve noon at the La Ópera cantina. Fucking Russian and his reactions! And that dead Chinaman cheerfully telling us everything about his plans. Fucking Chinaman! All about contraband morphine and the whole deal. And the Russian pretending he believed the whole damn thing. And the gringo not saying a word. Everyone believing what the Chinaman was saying, now all of them out there investigating. And now my neck hurts. Maybe that's my reaction, as the Russian says. Fucking Russian!

He stopped a taxi and gave him his address. At least I'll have time to take a shower. And see Marta. She's there in my house and I'm here acting like a chump with my international intrigues and my Outer Mongolia. I hope she closed the curtains. Those Russians have already seen too much. Must've seen more than I have. Fucking Russians!

V

When he entered the apartment, the dawn was spreading gray shadows everywhere, like large stains of mildew in an abandoned house. Nobody was there. Noiselessly, he opened the door to the bedroom. The colorless light entered the window, accompanied by the first noises from the street. Marta was sleeping, curled up, as if frightened, her bare arms outside the sheet and her hands joined next to her face. What those fucking Russians must have seen. They see everything because they're conducting an investigation, and I'm just around to kill. To kill without seeing what I'm killing, without knowing why I have to kill. Maybe just because.

He stopped to look at her. Her breathing was slow, unhurried. Without making a sound, he took off his jacket and holster. He didn't want to have it over his heart. Right now is when I should slip into bed with her. Right now when she's sleeping. I don't think I've ever seen a woman sleeping, at least not such a beautiful woman. Usually, by the time they fall asleep, I'm gone. I didn't need them anymore. I think I'm turning into a faggot. I should already be in bed with her. Why keep looking at what you can grab with both your hands? Fucking Russians across the street! Me only look, like the Chinamen would say, me no touch. And me just like them. Me not getting into bed. Fucking faggot!

He had absentmindedly picked up the chamois and was cleaning his gun. He moved his hand along it slowly, as if caressing it, but without taking his eyes off Marta sleeping in his bed. Without warning, she stirred, then bolted upright. All she had on was her slip.

"Filiberto!"

"Don't be afraid, Marta."

Marta rubbed her eyes and smiled:

"I waited up very late for you."

She made no move to cover herself with the sheet. She sat on the bed and placed both hands on her outstretched legs.

"Then I got sleepy and lay down for a while and ... I didn't have any pajamas ... Are you going to go to bed?"

"No, Marta. I just came home to take a shower. I have to go out again."

"But you haven't slept a wink. You haven't slept for two nights. Do you want some coffee?"

She leapt out of bed. She was barefoot. She walked up to García and placed both hands on his shoulders. Her breasts could be seen through her slip, small and hard, and her tussled hair fell to her shoulders. She smelled of body and bed. García leaned over and kissed her on the lips, without touching her. In one hand he had the gun and in the other the cloth. She pressed up against him.

"I love you, Filiberto, I love you very much. When I'm here alone I have nothing to do but think of you and how much I love you. That's why I'm telling you this now, because so much has changed in our relationship."

She took one step back and began to unbutton his shirt.

"You'll need a clean one."

"Yes, Marta."

"Why don't you rest a little? I'll wake you up whenever you tell me to."

"There's no time, Marta."

He gently moved her to one side and entered the bathroom. Fucking faggot! Me just standing there and her almost naked. That's what happens to old men. And I want her so bad ... Fucking faggot!

When he got out of the bathroom, his clean clothes were laid out on the bed. He began getting dressed. Marta appeared at the door holding a cup of coffee. García sat down on the bed. His legs were shaking.

"You can leave the coffee on the nightstand, Marta."

Marta put it on the nightstand and sat down on the bed, next to him.

"You're tired. You shouldn't work so much at night."

"This only happens once in a while, Marta. We are conducting a special investigation."

"You don't want to drink your coffee?"

García embraced her and kissed her, hard. His hands were shaking and there was a gaping pit in his stomach. They fell backward onto the bed. Marta smelled of the warm night, bed, and woman. García slowly got up, without taking his eyes off her.

"No, Marta, not like this. We'll have plenty of time when this is all over."

"Whenever you say, Filiberto. I'll be waiting for you. Whenever you say."

She smiled at him. If she smiles one more time, Mr. Rosendo del Valle and the colonel can both go fuck themselves. I'm such a fucking faggot! Since when have I been so damn polite when it comes to doing it with a bitch?

"You are a real man, Filiberto. That's why I love you so much. You don't want this to be something unimportant... I'll be here when you want me and however you want me, because you are a real man."

"Yes, Marta. Later..."

"I knew it the first time I saw you at the shop. Only a man like you, a real man, would do what you've done. When you said we should come to your house ... I knew what would happen ... But it didn't. You don't like it when things aren't done right, and that's why I love you. All day yesterday I thought about you ... You want me to put your shoes on?"

"No, thank you, Marta. I'll do it."

"I thought about you, about how you've behaved. You didn't just want to sleep with me ... like so many other man. You helped me and you didn't ask for anything in return ... and even now you're not asking for anything. But I'll be here, waiting for you ..."

"Yes, Marta."

He stood up and went over to the mirror to tie his silk tie. Then he put on his shoulder holster and over that his beige trench coat. He took out a dark-green silk handkerchief and placed it in his chest pocket. He turned to face Marta:

"I want you to go to Palacio de Hierro and buy yourself some dresses and anything else you need, Marta. You're not going back to Dolores Street..."

"No, never again."

"Here, there's six thousand pesos, take it ..."

"That's a lot of money."

"No, it's not. I want you to buy anything you want. Everything you see and like, buy it. That's what money's for."

144

"But ... how will I repay you for all this?"

She stood up from the bed and walked over to him. Her nipples were hard under her slip.

"How am I ever going to repay you for everything you've done for me?"

She took his hand and kissed it. García lifted her chin and kissed her on the mouth.

"There's the money. I might be back this afternoon."

"I'll be here."

"And when this is all over, we'll go to Cuautla, to Agua Hedionda, even to Acapulco. We'll take the car."

Marta smiled. There was great sweetness in her face.

"Whenever you want, Filiberto."

"Goodbye."

"Don't come back too late, Filiberto. You have to rest ..."

"Goodbye."

He left the apartment and went outside. The sun was beginning to paint the filth of the city a sickly yellow. Fucking faggot! I'm definitely out of my element. First with the gringo and the Russian and this international intrigue. And now with Marta. She's not like other women. Could it be because she's Chinese? Or she sees what a chump I am and they sent her to do her little job? And here I am, missing my chance to help her do it. Fucking dumbass! And she's even hotter than I thought. For all I know, by the time I get back, the job'll be over, and she'll leave with my money and all the rest of it. I'd have it coming to me for being a dumbass, for being the fucking dumbass that I am.

The professor lived on Arcos de Belén. Waking him up wasn't easy, and García had to bang on the door pretty hard. Finally, it opened. The stench in his room was nauseating.

"So early? What's gotten into you, Cap'n? Can't you see I'm nursing a bit of a hangover?"

"I've got a little job for you, Professor."

"Like the one yesterday?"

"I want you to find out everything you can about Luciano Manrique, the thug who had various sources of income."

"Luciano Manrique? I defended him once, Cap'n. But where he is now, according to the newspapers, even I can't get him out. Someone did him in, along with Villegas."

"Look, Professor, you know how things work as well as I do ..."

"I don't kill, I defend the accused. Acts of mercy ..."

"Guys like him, second-rate gunmen, they always have someone higher up who's protecting them, who pays for their lawyers ..."

"Priests also must partake of the altar ..."

"I want to know who was protecting this Manrique fellow, and who he was hanging around with lately. Find that out, and I'll give you another two hundred pesos."

"Another? You still haven't given me the first three hundred."

"Bring me the information at eleven, to La Ópera. Here's twenty on credit, for your expenses and to treat your hangover."

"Thanks, Cap'n. See you later."

The colonel, as always, was in a bad mood. Doesn't seem like the colonel ever sleeps. And it can't be because of his faithful departed, because he keeps his hands clean. Just like all of them who've come after us. They've all got clean hands because we do their dirty work for them. Fucking hands!

"Why did you strangle that gringa?"

"We found her dead, Colonel. The Chinks killed her because she was blackmailing them."

"Whenever you're involved in a case, the whole thing fills up with dead bodies. You never leave me anybody to interrogate."

"I didn't kill a single person last night."

"If you say so. Now, before Mr. del Valle gets here ... Those Chinese were lying to you. There are no drugs or money in the warehouses ..."

"No dollars?"

"Nothing. And based on what we've been able to find out from our informants, these people have not been in contact with any known drug traffickers. Even Villegas, according to what we know about him, had never been involved in that kind of business."

"I figured."

"Why?"

"As soon as we caught them, that older Chinaman, the one who seemed like the boss, he started to blab about the drugs and about moving in on the Mafia in the States. He was talking too much."

"So, what's their game? What we thought?"

"The Russian doesn't want to say anything, but I'm almost sure."

"Sure of what? It's harder to get information out of you than a criminal, García."

"I think the rumor the Russians heard in Outer Mongolia didn't have anything to do with an attack on the president of the United States. For one thing, there was too much money involved; for another, it wasn't well organized."

"So?"

"The Russians heard about something that's going to come down in Mexico, and they wanted a free hand to investigate."

"Something like what?"

García meditated for a moment. If I tell him what I think, he's going to say I've been smoking marijuana, but I've got to tell him, for silence means consent and that Russian with all his theories was treating me like I'm a moron.

"I didn't take you for an expert in international politics, García. I thought you applied your talents to purely regional problems."

"There are a lot of Cubans who don't like the Russians, and there are a lot of Chinamen in Cuba, Colonel. With a little help, they could plan a coup, throw out the Russians, and turn Cuba over to the Chinese."

"And?"

"And, the Russians wouldn't like that."

"I can imagine. And?"

"That was the rumor the Russians heard. They were preparing a counterrevolution, organized by the Chinese against the Russians in Cuba. And that counterrevolution was being prepared in Mexico, with money from Hong Kong."

"What about the report the Russians gave us?"

"They wanted our help, and especially the FBI's. With a story like that, we all had to work together to find out the truth."

The colonel reflected.

"So, according to you, García, there is no Chinese plot to assassinate the president of the United States?"

"I'm not absolutely sure, Colonel."

The colonel's face showed impatience. At that moment, the door opened and Mr. del Valle entered, his beatific smile playing on his lips and gleaming off his teeth. Both men stood up:

"Please, sit down, gentlemen."

He remained standing and began to talk as if he were giving a speech.

"I don't know if you realize that the president of the United States arrives tomorrow, and we still do not know what to expect. I am going to have to report to our president—"

The colonel cut him off. He recounted everything that had happened so far and explained García's theory that a Chinese plot against the Russians in Cuba was behind it all. Del Valle sat down to think. Then he asked:

"So, you are certain, Mr. García, that the only thing these Chinese want is a Chinese coup in Cuba?"

"I believe so."

"But are you absolutely certain?"

"There are too many people involved, Mr. del Valle. For an attack on the president of the United States, you don't need so many. All you need are a couple of well-trained fanatics. You also don't need that much money."

"I don't know," del Valle said. "Your arguments offer no proof. Let me ask you this: Are you sure that the lives of the two presidents are not in danger?"

"No."

"There you have it, Colonel—we can't be certain."

"Another thing that made me suspicious," García interrupted, "was the Russians' insistence on taking part in the investigation. It should have been enough for them to give us the warning."

"I believe, Colonel," del Valle said without paying any attention to García's words, "that there is something important going on among the Chinese, and, in light of the report from the Russian embassy, I believe that this something is a conspiracy to assassinate the president of the United States during his visit to Mexico—"

"But," said the colonel, "García explained—"

"Mr. García is not an expert in international intrigue. The truth is, he is not even an expert in police investigations. Much less can he accurately assess the Chinese and their well-known duplicity. I believe that, and I can even affirm that I am certain of it. Yes, absolutely certain. This investigation has not been properly conducted. Progress was made at first and a Chinese conspiracy was uncovered, but afterward, since yesterday, the investigation has taken a direction that I do not like."

"The investigation has gone where the investigation itself has led, Mr. del Valle," said the colonel.

"That direction is the wrong direction and has cost us time. The only sure thing is that the Chinese have received money. Unfortunately, given the methods used in this investigation, we have no witnesses. I notice a certain ... alacrity, shall we say, in the liquidation of possible witnesses."

García, his face expressionless, was holding his Stetson in both hands on his lap. So, Mr. del Valle is determined to believe in the Chinese threat and in this whole Outer Mongolia business. Fucking Outer Mongolia! And, fucking Mr. del Valle! We're liquidating all the witnesses, are we? If he doesn't like how I'm making my bricks, why doesn't he get in there and mix the clay?

"Moreover," del Valle continued, "the Americans have complained, tactfully of course, about Mr. García's attitude. They claim he is not being cooperative. Considering who Mr. García is, Colonel, considering his past, it's no wonder he's not used to teamwork, and this kind of investigation requires it."

The colonel did not reply. He was playing with his gold lighter. García remained impassive. Teamwork. To kill someone all you need is one man, not a team. A man who has balls and who's not afraid of blood. Fucking team! As if this were a soccer match. I draw my gun from the left, shoot to the right—*goal*, someone's been rubbed out for good.

Del Valle stood up again.

"Colonel, we have one day left to complete this investigation.

I want action, serious action, not the massacre of underlings, like the unfortunate event last night. I want the Chinese who are at the head of this conspiracy. I want to know where the money is and what it is going to be used for. And I want to know tonight, so I can tell Mr. President that he is no longer in any danger."

"We are doing everything we can. I have men investigating the Chinese connected with the Café Canton gang and the warehouses. We have increased surveillance of political exiles and along all our borders."

"It's not enough, Colonel."

"In the square where the statue is going to be unveiled, we have emptied out all the buildings that have balconies, and only people with special police passes will be able to get in. You, yourself, Mr. del Valle, signed those passes."

"It's not enough."

"We have recommended to the Americans that they use an armored car, to minimize the moments of danger."

"I'm telling you, Colonel, it's not enough. God in heaven, Colonel! What more do you want before you order a full-blown investigation? You already know the Chinese have received money; you know they are plotting something, and, putting aside Mr. García's bizarre and unfounded opinions, you know that that *something* is the assassination of the president of the United States. Hire some competent men, really competent, to move this investigation forward, like the FBI is doing. Can you imagine the embarrassment if a foreign police force discovered the truth before we did?"

"Yes, of course ..."

"Well, get going, then. We have only twelve hours left. Don't waste any more time on this nonsense. I feel certain that Mr.

García can keep himself otherwise occupied in the meantime. Good day."

Mr. del Valle opened the door and walked out with dignity. In the doorway, he stopped and turned back:

"Please, Mr. García, do not take this personally. I have no desire to offend you."

"García understands, Mr. del Valle."

"Of course, the Russian is an expert—"

"He uses a Luger," García interrupted. "I use a .45."

"What does that matter?"

"And the gringo uses a .38 police special. Maybe because they're experts. They know judo, karate, and how to strangle people with silk cords."

"I don't understand what you are getting at, Mr. García."

Mr. del Valle's voice was hard, curt, the voice of an official used to giving orders.

"Here in Mexico, they don't teach us all those skills. Here all they teach us is how to kill. Or maybe not even that. They hire us because we already know how to kill. We aren't experts, we're just amateurs."

There was silence. Mr. del Valle came back into the room. Fucking Mr. del Valle! What does he know anything about all of that? My hands smell of Marta. And I didn't even want to make out with her. Fucking faggot! Here, the one and only homo is Filiberto García, at your service.

"Look, Mr. García," said del Valle, "I had no desire to offend you. I admire the work you have done, but in such cases, sentimental considerations can play no part. It is not only the life of the president of the United States that is at risk, but the life of our president and world peace, as well. Based on your findings, you have reached the conclusion that the plot the Russians warned us about has some basis in fact. This is a big step, and it compels us to reach a very serious conclusion."

"I don't believe there is such a Chinese plot to assassinate the president of the United States."

"But you yourself said—"

"That there's a plot to bring Cuba into the Chinese sphere of influence."

"The evidence you've supplied is flimsy, Mr. García. In this case, you must defer to my long legal and administrative experience. You must defer to the investigations carried out by people who know how to do such things, the FBI and the KGB. Everything points to an attack being planned—"

"Yes," García interrupted. "I believe they are planning an attack, but not with the Chinese—"

"That is absurd! Don't you think, Colonel?"

"Yes, Mr. del Valle."

"So, given the little time we have, I don't want it wasted investigating this nonsense. We have only one day—one day, Colonel. Put your best men on this. If necessary, search all Chinese establishments in Mexico. That's an order, Colonel."

"Yes, sir."

"I think Mr. García has carried out the limited mission he was assigned and can now return to his regular occupations, whatever those may be."

"Yes, sir."

"Keep me informed of everything. Good day."

Mr. del Valle again opened the door, and this time he walked out. García had remained seated, staring at the wall in front of him. Now they've gone and cut me loose. Ugly. And I deserve all of it for being a dumbass and a bigmouth. Who told me to convince fucking del Valle of something he doesn't want to be convinced of? Better to be like the colonel. Yes, sir, Mr. del Valle, sir. Would you like me to kiss your ass, Mr. del Valle, sir? And I should return to my regular occupations. To my occupation as a hit man. We don't need hit men for this operation. When we need another stiff, we'll have you called in. But for now, don't bother, because we are working with a team. My hands don't smell like Marta anymore. Now you need a whole team to whack someone. I guess you also need a team to make it with a bitch. Fucking team!

"García."

"Yes, Colonel."

"You heard what Mr. del Valle said."

"I did."

"You were playing hardball, weren't you? What, did you *want* to get a rise out of him?"

"I'm going to take eight days off, Colonel."

"You are going to take exactly zero days off."

"I don't have anything to do with this anymore."

"What was that you said about another conspiracy?"

"Mr. del Valle doesn't believe it."

"Tell *me* about it."

"I don't know. But we've never investigated what Luciano Manrique was doing in my house. He had nothing to do with Villegas, who was a hired gun for the Chinese."

"Maybe it was something personal against you."

"That could also be."

The colonel walked over to the window and looked out, even though there wasn't anything to see. There must be a whole hell of a lot of people who've got something against me. But they'd want to pump me full of bullets. And Luciano, may he rest in peace, was up to something else, like giving me a warning. It's like the whole world knows I've turned into a faggot, and they think a club is enough to scare me off. And now, all the bereaved are going to come after me. Fucking bereaved! Looks like they'll have to wait till I die of old age to feel happy. Or as Gertruditas in Yurécuaro said: "Don't punish him. He's suffering enough on his own." Fucking Gertruditas! Seems she was right. The bereaved and all their suffering, but sometimes I think I'm the most screwed. Because now that the Revolution has become the government, even people wearing huaraches are digging their high heels into me. Fucking del Valle! Marta's probably already gone out shopping.

The colonel turned away from the window and walked back to his desk. García was still sitting in his chair, not moving, his hat on his lap. The colonel lit a cigarette. As usual, he didn't offer one.

"What do you think Luciano Manrique was looking for?"

"Don't know. Seems like it was some kind of warning. Like he wanted to let me know about something. But he didn't have time to give me the message."

"With you, they never have time for anything."

"So it seems."

"What message was it?"

"Could have been a warning, to let me know I was investigating something dangerous, to tell me not to get between the horse's legs. And they sent me that message the same night I was assigned to the job."

"I see. What else?"

"That message had nothing to do with the Chinese at Café Canton, or with the half a million dollars. It was something else."

"What?"

"To convince us that the Chinamen really do have evil plans, when, maybe, just maybe, it's someone else who does."

"I see."

The colonel was smoking in silence. Spoken out loud like that, the whole thing sounds pretty stupid, but I think that's just the point, we're starting to see that rat's tail. I would have loved to go with Marta to Palacio de Hierro. Buy this, Marta. And this one, too. Don't look at the price tag; if you like it, just buy it, don't look at the price. That's what we all do in life. We don't see what things cost.

"Could be," the colonel said, as if talking to himself, "that somebody, maybe even the Russians or some gringos, found out about the rumor and thought it would be the perfect opportunity to assassinate the president and blame the Chinese."

"Something like that, Colonel."

"Keep investigating."

"Yes, Colonel."

"And try to leave somebody alive for me to interrogate."

"I'll do my best."

"One more thing, García."

García had stood up and was starting to walk away, then stopped.

"You will report only to me. Understood?"

"Yes, Colonel."

He left and closed the door behind him. The colonel kept flipping the gold lighter between his fingers.

The hustle and bustle of the day was starting up on Dolores Street—shops were opening, the trash of the night was being taken away. Santiago was drinking a cup of tea.

"You want, Mr. García?"

"Thank you."

"Why you here so early in the street, Mr. García? Looking for bad guy?"

"Just passing through, Santiago."

"In China we say bad man never sleep because good man no let him."

"There's something to that."

"Have some tea, Mr. García."

"Any news around here?"

"Some, some."

Santiago leaned over to whisper in his ear. He smelled of garlic and opium.

"Honorable Mr. Liu very angry, very sad ..."

"What's wrong with him?"

"Marta. You remember Marta, Mr. García?"

"Yes."

"She Mr. Liu wife."

"His wife?"

"Second wife, as we say in China. And she run away. Since a few night, when you here, Mr. García."

"You don't say ..."

"Maybe you find her, Mr. García? Mr. Liu very *very* sad. Today he no open shop and he no talk to nobody."

"That's what you get for having two women, and at his age."

"Oh, this Chinese custom, very old Chinese custom, and very honorable. When wife very old, man take second wife so first wife can rest. Very honorable Chinese custom."

Santiago suddenly smiled, showing his few yellow teeth.

"You like Marta, Mr. García? Marta very pretty, very pretty."

"Did she have a sweetheart?"

"No, Mr. García. Honorable Mr. Liu never let her go out nowhere."

"But she did go out."

"Seem so, Mr. García. She leave and no come back."

"Have they looked for her?"

"Mr. Liu no want to speak to nobody. No want to open shop. Very sad, Mr. Liu, very sad."

"Maybe he's playing the part a little?"

"Maybe he love her, Mr. García. No good for man to put love into woman. Love like that for children, but no for woman, woman not loyal."

"That's why he's so sad?"

"To tell you truth, we no understand either, Mr. García. Juan Po and unhappy man talk last night. We no understand. But it like that. Maybe honorable Mr. Liu, after so many year here, he take some feeling from you people."

"Maybe."

"Drink your tea, Mr. García, tea from China, very good."

He took a sip. Fucking Chinamen. So you shouldn't love your woman, only your children, and those of us who don't have children, we're just screwed.

"Poor Mr. Liu do everything to make happy his women, but Marta very young and he more than fifty year old. This no good, Mr. García. Young people with young people."

"Yes."

"But, please, Mr. García, try to find Marta. It hurt to see feeling of honorable Liu and how he lose face in front of all honorable men because he have feeling. You look for her?"

"We'll see. Listen, Santiago, tell everybody to be very careful for a few days, to shut down the betting and the smoking ..."

"Danger?"

"Yes. I'll tell you when you can reopen."

"Much danger?"

"It'll pass, as always. But be very careful. See you soon."

"Goodbye, Mr. García, very honored for your visit, very honored."

He started walking toward the cantina. First Santiago acts

like Liu's the offended one and then, just like the gringo and the Russian, he starts investigating Marta. Might be pure love, might be pure distrust. Sounded like he was telling the truth. Fucking Liu! Maybe it's really tough on him that I took her away. He can go to hell. A girl like Marta shouldn't be with a man who's fifty. Maybe that's why I'm turning into a faggot. Maybe these fucking Chinks cast a spell on me, gave me the evil eye. And now all I can do is whisper sweet nothings in her ear. What will she buy? Maybe she's afraid to spend all those pesos. She doesn't know I'm on the trail of more of the same. 3-5-9-9-0-8. That's where the dough is, and I'm the only one who knows. Pretty clever.

He stopped at a tobacconist and dialed a number:

"Is this 3-5-9-9-0-8?"

"Yes."

"Mr. Wang?"

"There's no Mr. Wang here."

"This isn't his house?"

"No."

"Is this 3-5-9-9-0-8?"

"Yes."

They hung up. Very discrete, like they didn't want to say whose house it was. And it was a kid who answered. That's not a private home, and that wasn't a maid.

He dialed another number.

"Gomitos? García here."

"What's up, Captain?"

"I need you to find me an address."

"Orders from?"

"The colonel. It's the address with the phone number 3-5-9-9-0-8."

"I'll call you back in ten."

"I'll call you, Gomitos, and thanks."

He hung up. The bucks are there, all of them in green fifty-dollar bills. And seeing as how I don't work on a team, it'll all be for me. Fuck the team! Now we'll see who's a better investigator. Fucking investigation!

The professor was already in the cantina drinking his first tequila of the day, his tequila of salvation, as he called it, to be imbibed ritualistically, as if it were a sacrament. García took him over to a booth.

"Find out anything?"

"Luciano Manrique's exemplary life is an open book to me."

"What kind?"

"A somewhat pornographic book, like those novels they write these days, the ones they say are new art and very high-brow. Can I order another tequila, Cap'n?"

"Go ahead."

The professor ordered a double.

"Who was protecting Manrique?"

"Luciano Manrique's entire life, as well as his specific activities, can be reduced to one bit of legal terminology: chargeable offense. His name first appears in the Mexican police records of Tampico as a procurer: arrested for aggravated assault, charged with procuring and carrying illegal weapons—a club and assorted other bits. Three years. Released in two. He had learned an important lesson. If one wants to devote one's life to the professions of procurement, robbery, and similar activities, one must be allied with some member of the police force. So he becomes a policeman in Tamaulipas. As you can see, Cap'n, and without meaning any offense, he rose in the criminal ranks while sinking deeper into the swamp."

"Who got him out of jail?"

"He became buddies with a policeman, who in turn became buddies with the chief of military operations, one General Miraflores. Cheers, Cap'n."

"Why did he get him out?"

"Perhaps out of noble feelings of mercy for his fellow human beings, Christian mercy. Though if that were the case, it would be the only instance of such feelings in General Miraflores's brilliant career. There are those with malevolent but probably correct notions who claim that Miraflores had him released from jail so he could help him collect his cut from the local prostitutes."

"Then what?"

"When the general came to Mexico City and Mr. Rosendo del Valle left the government of Tamaulipas, Luciano came, too, and apparently without a job title. Just in case, as they say. He brought with him his wife, or mistress or consort, with whom he lived on Camelia Street, number 87."

"Has in been in jail here in Mexico City?"

"Once, for robbery. He got out on bail thanks to his brilliant defense attorney, your humble servant."

"And who paid for your services?"

"His wife. Again, they caught him with a stolen car. But they couldn't prove anything, and the owner of the car, thanks to my efforts, withdrew the complaint."

"Who paid you, Professor?"

"The wife."

"Where did she get the money?"

"You want hearsay?"

"Yes."

"General Miraflores. Seems he was very fond of our man. I was, too, and he was turning out to be a good client, until … until he died."

"What else?"

"The woman's name is Ester Ramírez. She was working at a whorehouse in Tampico, and Luciano Manrique rescued her from that ignominious and degraded life. So, what about my fee, Cap'n?"

"Here."

"Thank you. I see you subtracted the thirty pesos."

"I did. That was the deal."

"Okay, okay. In fact, Cap'n, the police still haven't found out who murdered the men in the black Pontiac, as they are now called in the newspapers."

"So?"

"But in the courts, word has it that the police know who killed them but orders have come from higher up to drop the investigation. Cheers, Cap'n."

"And lately, just before he died, is anything known about what Manrique was doing?"

"He had more money than usual and was often seen in the company of new friends."

"Who?"

"One they call the Toad. He's also from Tampico, and he also worked with the police there. The other one, according to what they say, is a recently arrived gringo who lives in a hotel on Mina Street. And, it seems, there's been a whole new wave of crimes. Last night, they found four men and a woman, dead, in a room on Guerrero Street."

"Really."

"Turns out the woman was the inconsolable widow you and I interviewed yesterday afternoon. She was strangled with an electrical cord."

"Really."

"They must have killed her shortly after we left."

"I left her with you, Professor."

The professor took a sip of tequila, then smiled.

"We both live from crime, Cap'n, but those of my profession have reached the conclusion that killing our potential clients is not only unethical but very bad business. In the circles you move in, on the other hand, one has not reached this conclusion."

"You're crossing a line, Professor."

García's voice did not sound hard, only tired. The professor smiled again.

"Don't get mad, Cap'n. It was only a joke. Cheers."

"Cheers."

The professor finished his tequila and ordered another. Fucking jokes. Fucking truth. So we're dumbasses because we kill our clientele. Maybe only chumps work in this business—the sharp-witted ones study law. And what about the Russian and the gringo? Seems they studied their profession, like the professor. And I didn't study shit. I fell into it without even knowing why or how. Maybe because it was there for the taking. Or because that was life in those days. Or because that's how they wanted me to be. Fucking life! And the gringo and the Russian studied a lot to become what I am. And this lawyer, what is he? A cantina rat? Specialists, del Valle said. Fucking gunslingers like me! And now Marta comes along and tells me how good I am! What the fuck?! What would the professor say if I told him that? Good Filiberto. Fucking faggot Filiberto! What would he say if I told him about Marta? There should be a university department for gunslingers. Experts in slinging guns. Experts in screwing others over. Experts in churning out the faithful departed. One year of studies to learn not to remember the dead you leave behind. And another year, so that even if you do remember, you don't give a damn. Does this lawyer remember all the dirty cases he's been in on? All the bribes? They say some killers notch their guns for each of their victims. Dumbasses! I don't need to make any marks to remember. For all I know Graves made a mark on his gun last night. Or maybe he keeps a list. That Russian with his reactions. If after every killing, he ate like he said he does, he'd be fat as hell. And he says Graves goes and tells all, like in confession. And Marta confesses to me. All that's left is for me to have the urge to confess to her. Fucking confession! There are things you never tell anybody. Hey, Marta, one day in Parral I killed a woman. She was making a chump out of me and I killed her. Hey, Marta, out in Huasteca, I strangled an old man with an electrical cord. And in Mazatlán, I whacked two guys in a cantina. First I got them drunk. There they were, slumped over on the floor, backs against the counter, their eyes wide open. The dead always have stupid expressions on their faces. And me pretending to be good old Filiberto. Listen, Marta, out there in San Andrés Tuxtle, I killed a man then fucked his wife, right there in the same room, I raped her. Must have been one of those reactions the Russian was talking about. Because now those things aren't low-down shit, they're reactions. The Russian police even keeps lists of them: after killing, Filiberto García is known to rape the victim's wife.

"You angry, Cap'n?"

"No, Professor. Actually, there's a question I've been wanting to ask you for a long time."

"Ask away, Cap'n. Another tequila, Raymundo!"

"You studied at the university and received your law degree."

"In 1929. If you want, I can show you my certificate. I must have it around, somewhere."

"With all that, your studies and your degree, it doesn't seem like you've gotten very far, have you?"

"That hurt your feelings, didn't it, what I said before?"

"No, it's not that. But I've heard that you know everything there is to know about the law."

"Summa cum laude. But it didn't do me much good, did it? Thanks, Raymundo. This one's to your health, Cap'n. Maybe it was true what my father said. He was also a lawyer: 'What nature doesn't give, Salamanca won't provide.'"

He finished his tequila in one gulp. When he spoke again there was a strange sadness in his voice.

"My father was a lawyer and a supporter of Porfirio Díaz. Always wore a bowler hat and a suit. He was a judge and they said he'd be a magistrate. Don Porfirio was his friend. But he didn't become a magistrate; he didn't become anything. You know why, Cap'n?"

"Because of the Revolution?"

"No. Many like him, including one of his closest friends, joined the Revolution. But my father remained loyal. He resigned. He wouldn't serve a rebel government of mutinous officers and the masses. He resigned and then he wasn't nothing or nobody. He could recite the laws in Latin and he spoke French and German, but he wasn't nothing or nobody, because he wanted to remain loyal. The old fool."

"Don't talk like that, Professor."

"But I started working as a lawyer during the time when the military was in charge. The days of men like you, Cap'n. The military and the law don't get along very well. More important than knowing all the articles of the Code, and all the Latin phrases my father taught me, was getting in good with some general, with one of our many heroes. Because there's one thing you learn from military men: being right isn't worth shit, what matters is having buddies. Just look at the case of Luciano Manrique."

"He's dead, Professor."

"That's right—he got unbuddied. But as it turns out, a lawyer who's nobody's buddy is one lawyer too many in this buddiocracy. Now that I think about it, my father was loyal to Don Porfirio, but I couldn't be loyal to the law I studied. Instead of justice, I was looking for buddies. It's what would've happened to you, Cap'n, if you'd been young when there were lots of laws in the land."

The professor grew quiet. A stupid smile hovered over his lips. Fucking professor! It's like he's pulling my leg. With this guy you never know. He has absolutely no fear, but he doesn't have any balls, either. Maybe because he's a drunk. Or because by now he doesn't give a rat's ass. And the Russian said he was going to come at noon. For all I know he won't come because they already told him I'm no expert. He's probably busy doing something with all his technology. With his international intrigue. Waiting for messages from the far reaches of Outer Mongolia. Fucking Outer Mongolia!

The professor raised his hand to get Raymundo's attention.

"Another tequila, Raymundo. And as time passed, Cap'n, I learned to make buddies, but I didn't forget the law. And since you didn't have to go to the university to make buddies, just the cantina, I became a drunk. But you, Cap'n, you had lots of opportunities when you were young, so you never became a drunk. And now that we're living in a lawyerocracy, I'm already too buddified to be worth anything to anybody. Cheers, Cap'n."

"Cheers, Professor."

He drank the shot of tequila that had been placed in front of him. A small shot, like for a bird.

"And in order to live, I have to work with my buddies, with people like you, like the ones from my early days. In this way,

I'm just like my father who remained loyal to Don Porfirio. I'm loyal to all of you. And that's why, like my father, I'm so screwed."

Laski entered the cantina. García signaled to him to come over, and he let the professor know he should move to a different table. The professor picked up his glass, put back on his stupid and complacent smile, and went over to the bar. Laski approached.

"What's up, Filiberto, my friend?"

"I thought you wouldn't come."

"Because you're no longer working on our case? You have a very poor concept of friendship, Filiberto."

"What happened to all that crap about feelings?"

"That is true. We have no feelings. But we can greet our good friends."

He sat down and ordered a beer.

"It's going to be very bad for me," he said.

"Why drink it, then?"

"One thing I've learned in Mexico: cantinas have very bad milk. Yet another proof of how ancient Mexican culture is."

Laski tasted his beer.

"Any more news from Outer Mongolia?"

"No. But I'm very interested in your theory about the Cubans and the Chinese, Filiberto?"

"Really?"

"And I'm thinking it's time we leave in the efficient hands of our friend Graves the protection of his president and we, Filiberto, my friend, we investigate to find out whatever truth might be behind your theory."

"Why me? I think I will also leave in your capable hands the defense of Russian interests in Cuba. I've got other things to do."

"Like going to Cuautla with Miss Fong?"

"Among other things."

"And you don't want to find out if your theories are correct?"

"I already know."

"You don't want to know where all those dollars are?"

"They're not mine. They belong to the Chinese ... and you people."

"But they're there and there's no clear owner."

"You knew that money was for carrying out a coup in Cuba, didn't you?"

"We considered that possibility. Don't you want to work with us, Filiberto?"

"I've already got a job."

"You have to go to Cuautla with Miss Fong."

"That's none of your business."

"You haven't slept in two nights and you're tired, Filiberto. But I want you to consider my proposition. As well as the five hundred thousand dollars hanging around, somewhere, with no owner."

"There's no reason to consider either, Ivan Mikhailovich. I'm sick and tired of this shit about Outer Mongolia and Constantinople and the whole damn business. I've never had anything to do with international intrigue, and I don't want to start now."

Laski sat staring at him. There was great sadness in his eyes.

"Filiberto, my friend, *tovarich*, I know what's going on with you. We offended you the other night, when Graves and I were talking about our old adventures. But I assure you, our intentions were not to ... to embarrass you, let us say. I know that some of your adventures leave all mine in the dust, and that's why we want your help."

"I have a job."

"For example, what you did there in that training camp that had been set up in Chiapas …"

"What do you know about that?"

"We were very upset about the whole affair. That camp could have become very important, and you destroyed everything. We never thought anybody could find it, but we didn't count on your nose and your courage, Filiberto. And we thought that you would only, at the worst, arrest the boys. Why did you kill them?"

"Because I don't like to be the dead one. Did you train those men?"

"They were good infiltrators. When you killed them, certain people in the highest places considered putting you on a list of those to be liquidated. Good thing we didn't."

"See you around, Ivan Mikhailovich."

"I'll ask you again, in two or three days, when this whole fuss about the presidential visit is over."

"Don't waste your time."

García stopped at the tobacconist, picked up the public telephone, and dialed a number:

"Gomitos? García here."

"I've got the information you asked for, Cap'n. You sure the colonel's not going to be pissed off?"

"Sure."

"The telephone number you gave me is in a house on Dolores Street, under the name of Hong Kong Pacific Enterprises."

"What address on Dolores?"

"Number 189. No apartment number. There's something else."

"What?"

"It was installed just two weeks ago."

"Thanks, Gomitos. See you later."

"If the colonel asks . . . ?"

"He's got no reason to ask you anything, but if he does, tell him you gave me the information."

He hung up the phone and hopped on a bus. Useless to wait for a taxi. I should've brought the car, but then, where would I park it. Fucking colonel doesn't want me to use special plates. And all that dough on Dolores Streets, so close to where I'm going now. And now the Russian wants me to work with him. How many agents does he have on this thing? Some we know about, and the others are playing very earnestly at being tourists. And del Valle's shit about how I'm no expert, so now the real experts want to hire me. Marta must've already returned from her shopping spree. I feel like telling them all to go to hell and getting into bed. Why should I give a shit if they kill the gringos' president? And what do I care about world peace? Tomorrow at this time we'll know if they whacked the president or not. But the gringos will have rolled out all their security. They're the experts. Like they were in Dallas. And me, maybe tonight I'll show up on Dolores Street. If I had all that dough, what the hell would I care what happens? And that fucking professor with all his memories. Seems we're all having a go at our memories and our confessions. So he wasn't loyal to his laws. Fucking laws! Laws are for dumbasses, not for us and not for the lawyers. It's like they just stole the Revolution right out of our hands. But I never had it in my hands. Those who are born in the gutter . . . General Miraflores scaled the heights, but now these lawyer-types have left even him in the dust.

The house on Camelia Street turned out to be a run-down tenement. He knocked on the door of the room they directed him to and a thin woman with large dark eyes dressed in black opened it.

"Ester Ramírez?"

"What do you want?"

"Police."

"Come in."

They entered the small room with wood floors painted what they call *Congo yellow*. You could tell the woman had done the impossible to make it look like a living room, with two small rickety tables covered with embroidered tablecloths and porcelain figurines, these probably taken from some old inn out in the boondocks. There were even curtains, but all that effort to disguise the poverty made it stand out more.

"Have a seat," the woman said.

García took off his hat and sat down on one of the chairs. The woman sat in the other. This broad has been crying her eyes out. Maybe she really felt for the dead man. And now it's like she's all empty inside, like she doesn't have anything left at all.

"What can I do for you?"

"I want to talk to you about Luciano Manrique."

"Why? I already told the police everything I know and he ... he's dead. What for?"

"Did you tell the police about the Toad and the gringo?"

"I don't know who they are."

"It might have been them who killed Luciano. They were his buddies ... the Toad was in the police with him, back home."

"Yes."

"You knew him.

"Yes. He was a bad man."

"And a friend of Luciano's?"

"I told him not to be friends with him anymore. He was a bad man, a professional hit man. Luciano never killed anybody, never ..."

"But he was in jail."

"Yes. And I worked in a whorehouse and that's why we could never live in peace. That's why we had no right to anything. I don't even have the right to be alone in my own house, thinking about him, about that man who was so good to me, the man I loved. It must sound funny to you, doesn't it? A woman from a whorehouse who loves a man? Pretty funny, eh?"

"No."

"My love for Luciano, it was the only thing I had. The only thing, you understand? And now that's gone. And I can't even be alone in my house and think about him."

"What business did he have with the gringo?"

"I don't know anything about his business, and I don't want to. Luciano was good, but he was weak and he was ambitious. He said he wanted to give me lots of things and, sometimes, when he had money, he gave me things. I didn't ask for anything, only that he be here and be good, but he wanted to give me things, he wanted to be important. I begged him for so long to take a job. We didn't need much. General Miraflores would have given him a steady job, but he didn't want one. He was looking for something else ... And now he's dead."

"He talked about making a lot of money?"

"He was always talking about that, but I'd stopped listening. 'Go pick out your car,' he'd tell me. 'This deal can't go wrong.' 'We're going to live in our own house.' That's how he'd talk to me, because he loved me, because he was good to me, but I knew it would never happen. I stopped even trying to get him to forget about all those things. I just kept loving him, that's all."

García remained quiet. Fucking broad! She's going to keep talking about her dearly departed, as if any of that mattered. They say that Filiberto García rapes the widows of the men he kills. But now he's a faggot.

"I should've insisted, I should've threatened to leave him, but he took me out of the whorehouse, so he never listened to me, he didn't think what I said mattered. And that's true, he took me out of the whorehouse—he was good to me."

"Lately, did he have more money than usual?"

"I don't know. Sometimes. A week ago he gave me some to pay the three months rent we owed and the bill at the grocery store. And he bought me a pair of stockings. That's how he was. But now they've gone and killed him. And the police don't want to tell me anything. They just wanted me to identify the body. The night before last I waited up for him all night and only yesterday afternoon did they come to tell me. That's how you are, you policemen. And then I talked to General Miraflores, who's helped us so many times. I just wanted them to give me his body so I could hold a wake and bury him. But he didn't want to do anything, he didn't even want to talk to me. That's what his assistant said, that the general didn't want to talk to me and that he had nothing to do with Luciano. Fair weather friends."

"Who hired him for the job he was doing?"

"I don't know what he was doing. He said it was something big, very big. That's what he said. I didn't want him to get involved in those big things, but he never paid any attention to what I said. We've never had anything to do with those big things, they aren't for us. We deal in small things, things for people who did time or who worked in a whorehouse. And now he's dead, sir, dead, and the person who killed him, what did he know about how good he was to me? What did he know about the things he said to me? What did he know about how he took me out of the whorehouse because I was so unhappy there, because I was never happy there? But that's something they don't understand, men who kill. They don't realize, when they do that, that there's no going back."

"You want to find out who killed him and why?"

"What for? A man killed him ..."

"You don't want to know who?"

"A man."

"And if it was the Toad and that gringo who lives there in that hotel on Mina Street?"

"What does it matter?"

"You don't want them to be punished?"

"What does it matter? Look, sir, I know he was nobody important. But he was a man and he had the right to live, like you do and like I do. And they killed him. And he'd never killed anybody. He might have been a thief, he might have been a crook, like they say, but he wasn't a gunman, he wasn't a hit man. He didn't even own a gun. Just a club, to defend himself. He did bad things, but who hasn't? But he didn't have blood on his hands. And they killed him."

"What about the gringo?"

"I told Luciano not to have anything to do with him. But he told me we were never going to be poor again, we were going to be important people. 'You can't imagine all the things we'll do, Mrs. Manrique,' that's how he talked to me because he was good to me. We weren't married, but when he was happy he always called me Mrs. Manrique. He even said we were going to get married and we were going to live in our own house, in Chihuahua. He was going to hunt deer. He even had a rifle."

"Is it here?"

"What?"

"The rifle?"

"No, the gringo has it. He brought it across the border."

"Had Luciano ever been a hunter?"

"No, but he was going to be. He told me that when he was a boy, the men would take him along. Sometimes he was like a child. He lived on dreams, on his desire to do things they told him important people did, like hunting. And four days ago, he brought a rifle to show me. I don't think he even knew how to use it, but he was very happy with it. He told me the gringo was going to give it to him."

"What was it like?"

"I don't know anything about those things. It had a lens on top of the barrel and he told me to look through it. He was like a child."

They sat in silence. Fucking child! Playing with the rifle they were going to use to kill the president of the United States. But now he's dead. I figure Marta wouldn't understand these things. Even though she said she saw a lot of things there in Canton. But those are Outer Mongolian things. Fucking Outer Mongolia!

"You don't know if he had any Chinese friends from around here?"

"No. I never heard him talk about any of them. Not even the Chinaman from the coffee shop on the corner. Luciano was mad at him because he didn't want to let us have credit."

"And the Toad? When did he come around?"

"About two weeks ago, or less. He came to talk him into something. I never trusted that man. I know he's a bad one. Once, in Tampico, he killed one of the girls in the whorehouse. For no reason. He's mean. And I told Luciano, but his head was turned by the money they offered him and with the idea of buying me a house in Chihuahua. That's how he was. He wanted everything for me, and now they went and killed him."

"What did the Toad want to talk him into?"

"I don't know. Something big. Along with that gringo. Poor Luciano had always wanted to do something big."

"Do you need money, Ester?"

"For what?"

"There are always expenses. Here, I'm going to give you five hundred pesos."

He left the house. Ester sat there, the bill in her hand, not aware of anything. I'm a fucking dumbass! But one day, I could tell this to Marta. No, on second thought.... She saw the dead man, she saw the knife. She won't understand this. I threw away five hundred pesos, and I don't even know why. Here I am, once again, thinking I'm in a soap opera. She'd already told me what I wanted to know, without me giving her any money. But there goes the chump again. "Here, take, five hundred pesos, buy whatever you want." I don't even know if she realized I put it in her hand. Fucking dumbass!

At the third hotel he visited on Mina Street, he came upon the name of the American. Edmund T. Browning, from Amarillo, Texas. Tourist. He was the only gringo tourist registered, and it looked like Magallanes Hotel didn't get many foreigners. The receptionist, a thin young man, neatly dressed with big dark eyes and a full head of shining, well-groomed hair, was obviously nervous:

"We've never had any problems with the police, sir. This is a family hotel ..."

"Yeah, to make families," García said.

The receptionist looked at him with sadness and disgust. He's got a limp wrist. Butters his bread on the wrong side.

"When did Browning get here?"

"Six days ago. He seems like a responsible man, very polite."

"Where's he from?"

"The States. He came in his car, and I myself gave him room 328. He wanted an inside room, without windows on the street, because of the noise. He's very sensitive."

"What car does he drive?"

"A beautiful Chevrolet. Impala, brand new."

"Is he in his room?"

"No, he went out."

"Give me the key."

"I don't know if I should, sir …"

García grabbed his tie and almost lifted him out from behind the counter.

"You have no right."

"Give me the key."

"You have no right, I'm going to complain—"

García slapped him with his left hand. The receptionist exuded the scent of a sickly sweet perfume.

"No right," he said, his eyes filling with tears.

García abruptly released him and pushed him backward. He fell to the floor, banging his head against the wall filled with pigeonholes for the room keys. Blood dribbled out of the corner of his mouth. García reached over and took the key to room 328. The receptionist looked at him, his eyes filled with hatred.

The elevator stopped on the third floor. Room 328 was to the right—300 to 325 to the left, 326 to 340 to the right. García knocked on the door, waited a moment, then opened it. Mr. Browning was a very neat and methodical man. Two suits were hanging in the closet, and there was a hunting rifle with its telescopic sight in its leather case. On the shelf above the closet was a box with twenty-eight rifle cartridges. García took the weapon out of its case. Fucking gringo! He sure knows how to take care of a weapon. It's well oiled. But he hasn't used it much. All dressed up and ready to go, as they say. A gift for his Latin American friend, Luciano Manrique. So, they didn't see this at customs. Maybe it didn't even pass through customs.

The tools for cleaning the rifle were in a bag in the case—rags, a small brush, and a can of 3-in-One Oil. MADE IN MEXICO.

He put everything back in its place, walked out, and locked the door. When he got downstairs, the receptionist had already cleaned the blood off his face and combed his hair. He seemed on the verge of tears.

"Here's the key, my friend."

"Thank you."

"Tell Browning the police were here."

"Yes, I will."

"One more thing, my friend . . ."

The receptionist pushed himself back against the wall, as far away from García as possible.

"Does Mr. Browning ever have any visitors?"

"I don't know, sir."

García stretched his hand out toward him. The receptionist saw it coming but did nothing to stop him. The hand again grabbed his tie and pulled.

"Two gentlemen came . . ."

"That's better. Nobody can say you don't cooperate with the police, my friend. What are the visitors' names?"

"Truth is, I don't know, sir. I swear I don't. They never told me."

"One of them is about as tall as me, dark, heavyset, with bulging eyes, right?

"Yes. He's the one who comes most often."

García let go of his tie. The receptionist fell back against the wall. He looked over at the door with despair in his eyes, as if hoping somebody would show up.

"Thank you, my friend. And next time, be a little faster with your information. Or are you the type who likes it a little rough?"

"No, sir, no. And that ... you have no right ..."

"You're right, my friend, I have no right. Who else comes to visit him?"

"The other man, he's short, thin, always wears a trench coat."

"What about women?"

"We don't allow ..."

"Women?"

The receptionist was getting more and more nervous. His eyes were filling with tears. García's hand was again reaching out for him.

"He's got a woman in room 311."

"Let's go pay her a visit."

"But no, sir ... I can't leave my post. My assistant went to eat and won't be back till—"

"Let's go. Bring your master key."

The receptionist looked from side to side, hoping for somebody to rescue him, but there was nobody. He took a key attached to a chain with a large plastic bar out from under the counter and walked into the hallway. García grabbed him by the arm and could feel he was shaking. Fucking faggot! He's more afraid than a rabbit in a fox hole. But nicely perfumed.

They stopped in front of room 311.

"Open it."

"Shouldn't we knock first? The lady might be ... She might not be fully dressed."

The pressure on his arm increased.

"I don't see why a naked woman would bother you any, my friend. Open it."

He opened the door. A female voice called out from inside the room:

"Who's there? Oh, it's you, Mauricio! You should knock before entering ..."

She fell silent when she saw García following Mauricio into the room. The woman was lying in bed, half her body covered by the sheet, the other half, naked. Her hair was a mess and she wasn't wearing any makeup. When she saw García, she quickly pulled the sheet up to cover her firm, heavy breasts. She must have been about thirty, with fine features, large blue eyes, and an aquiline nose. Her face didn't match the heaviness of her breasts.

"Who's that man?" she asked.

"Don't be afraid, honey."

"I can't receive anybody. Mauricio, how dare you bring that man in here? You know I can't receive anybody..."

García came up right to the edge of the bed, then stopped and stared at her. His eyes were hard, emotionless. The woman had to lift her eyes to look him in the face, which made her look like she was begging.

"I'm telling you, I can't—"

"Shut up!"

"But it's just that—"

"I told you to shut up."

"It's just ... I think there's been a mistake. I can't attend to you. Edmund might come at any moment and—"

"What do you know about that gringo?"

"Edmund?"

"Yeah."

"He's my friend. Is that a crime?"

"What's he doing here in Mexico?"

"He's a tourist, sightseeing. And he's got the money for it."

"What else is he doing?"

"What do I know? And you, who the hell are you? I'm going to tell Edmund when he comes—"

With his left hand, García pushed her back against the pillow and with his right he grabbed her breast and started to squeeze and twist it. The woman wanted to shout, but he covered her mouth with his hand.

"What's the gringo doing in Mexico?"

Tears rolled down the woman's cheeks. García kept squeezing her breast, harder and harder. He took his hand away from her mouth. Mauricio's eyes were popping out of his head, and saliva was dribbling out of his open mouth.

"What's the gringo doing here?"

"Let me go, please let go. I didn't know him before, I swear, I'd never met him. He hired me to keep him company... Please, let go, you're hurting me ... Damn gringo. I don't know why he wants me here. He's never here ... Please, sir, let me go ..."

García let go. The woman covered her breasts. She took quick, shallow breaths, like she was aroused. She tried to smile.

"Thank you," she said.

She didn't rub her hurt breast. She stared at García.

"Where does he go when he goes out?"

"I don't know. Why don't you tell Mauricio to leave? Three's a crowd—"

"Does he go out with his friends?"

"Yeah. With that guy they call the Toad and another one ... Sometimes he comes back very late, but he's never drunk. Tell Mauricio—"

"Do you go out with him?"

"I did once. He took me for a ride in his car. I wanted to go to Chapultepec, or El Pedregal ... But instead he took me to that plaza where they're putting up the Statue of Friendship. I don't know what he wanted to see there, but he kept driving around and around and around, without saying a word. Please, tell Mauricio ..."

Now she was rubbing her hurt breast, not to relieve the pain but rather unconsciously, sensually.

"Tell Mauricio, please. Three's a crowd ..."

"Just the two of you were in the car?"

"Tell Mauricio—"

"Just you two alone?"

"Listen, after all, who do you think you are, you bastard? Get the hell out of here before ..."

García leaned over her and pulled the sheet up over her breasts. Then he turned to the receptionist.

"Let's go, Mauricio."

They left, closing the door behind them. The woman started crying. In the hallway, Mauricio dared open his mouth. His hands were shaking:

"Mr. Browning is going to get very angry and Doris will probably tell him everything."

"Did you get Doris for him?"

"No!"

"You got her, didn't you?" García's hand was squeezing his arm hard, pressing his skin against the bone.

"I ... I introduced them."

"He asked for a woman?"

"He told me ... that he wanted to meet someone. So I introduced him to Doris ..."

They went down in the elevator. Mauricio ran to take refuge behind the counter. García walked up to him:

"I think, my friend, that it would be better not to tell the gringo anything. He's not going to be here for long."

"Yes, sir ..."

He went out and found a public telephone.

"García here, Colonel."

"More dead?"

"No. I have to see you. I think I've come across something important."

"Come here."

"Maybe it would be better not to meet in your office, Colonel. You'll soon understand why."

"Where are you?"

"On Mina Street, Hotel Magallanes."

"That's almost at the corner of Guerrero. Wait for me on the corner. I'll come in my car, the Mercedes."

"Very well, Colonel."

He walked to the corner. It was two thirty in the afternoon. Not even twenty-four hours left, but now we're seeing the whole stinking rat. Fucking Outer Mongolia! I think I'm being followed. I've seen that guy twice already. Fucking Russian! Thought he was going to play me for a chump with his team and his technology and his Outer Mongolia. And them leading us around by the nose with their Chinks and their dollars from Hong Kong. This is what they call a smoke screen in war. Fucking smoke screen! And behind the screen the clever ones are getting away with murder. Absolutely sure they've already seen our backsides. With their rifles with telescopic sights. They think they're in Dallas. But they don't know what it takes to kill a president. Here, if you want to do that, you've got to be right on the spot, right where he is. And then you have to die there, too. That guy is definitely tailing me, and seeing as how I'm not going anywhere, he's fucked, he doesn't know what to do. Let him tail me. I'm done with this mess. I'll just turn it over to the colonel and take myself home. To Marta, to take a look at what she's bought. Maybe I'll even buy something for her. Because now we're finally done with the daytime soap. Now we're going to get serious, and we'll do it because we both want to do it. Like things should be done and not like I've always done them before. And that's why I'm going to bring Marta something. A brooch, or maybe a watch. She doesn't have a watch. Fucking Chink Liu! And maybe before going home, I'll go around to Dolores Street, have a look at where they've stashed the dough. Then I'll go back at night. Fucking Doris! If I hadn't been in such a hurry, who knows. And if it hadn't been for Marta. But she was a looker. And it seemed like she even liked my touch. Those sick bitches! I was liking it, too. Why not admit it? But now, when I get home, I'll be with Marta and then I'll take her out to dinner before going for the dough. I'll take her out in the car. To Las Lomas. And tomorrow, Cuautla, and maybe even Acapulco. She must look smoking hot in a bathing suit. And she'll love it. I don't think she's ever been sightseeing. Fucking Chink Liu! And that del Valle, telling me this is only for experts. He's right. What he doesn't know is that the real expert is me, his minion, that motherfucker. Because Outer Mongolia, it moves me as much as a gust of wind did that statue of Juárez: not one fucking inch.

VI

The colonel stopped at the corner.

"Get in, García."

He drove off.

"What's going on?"

"I think we've nailed it, Colonel."

He told him what he'd done during the day.

"Did you take the rifle?"

"No, I didn't want to alarm them, Colonel."

The colonel drove along in silence. He was thinking hard. He took out a cigarette and lit it. He blew the smoke out slowly. He turned down a side street and stopped the car. García turned around, looking for the person following him.

"Why couldn't you tell me this in the office?"

"Because there we wouldn't know who's listening. If the people I suspect are the ones involved in this, they could and probably do have spies in your office, Colonel."

"Could be. Someone told Manrique that you were on the case."

"Right."

"Couldn't it be the Russians themselves, like you suspected before? And they're using the opportunity because they think we'll blame the Chinese."

"I don't think so, Colonel. Those Russians know how to organize things. They don't use local talent like Luciano Manrique or the Toad. This is local. Now it's clear, the target isn't the gringos' president, it's ours. Using the rumors as their opportunity, Colonel."

The colonel kept smoking in silence. This notion is spinning around in his head faster than a mouse on his wheel. For all I know he's trying to figure out which side he should be on.

"What you're telling me is dangerous, García."

"That's why I wanted to tell you where nobody would hear."

"If it's true, the people implicated are very high up, very high, indeed. Do you understand?"

"Yes."

"And we have to tread very carefully."

"There's not much time left, Colonel."

"No, not much. How do you think they're planning on carrying it out?"

"Easy. They give police passes to the Toad and the gringo and place them among the guards in the square. They use the rifle."

The colonel picked up the car radio and spoke. He gave orders for a guard to be placed at the Magallanes Hotel and for the arrest of the gringo, Browning, and the Toad. He also ordered the rifle be confiscated from Browning's room.

"They probably have other weapons available, Colonel. And even other men."

"Right."

"Have to go the top, the tip-top."

The colonel was thinking.

"You are absolutely sure of your facts?"

"Yes."

García lit a cigarette. The colonel wants me to be the one to say that I'll take care of the fat cats, on my own. Out of loyalty. So if things go wrong, they'll say it was that dumbass García who's to blame, and they'll screw me. But they already know it's me. No orders, nothing.

"It's probably better not to tell the FBI," the colonel said, "and definitely not to ask them for help. We need people we can trust."

"Yes, Colonel."

"I don't have anybody I can trust to watch the principals. It's a very delicate task."

"For experts, Colonel."

The colonel glanced at him. A light smile was hovering over his lips. Fucking colonel! He doesn't want to give the order. And in the meantime, I can play the chump. If he wants me to whack those sonsabitches, he's going to have to say so. But I don't have any experience with that kind of thing. They would be proper corpses, and I only know how to make stiffs.

"Ever since Obregón," the colonel suddenly said.

Yeah. Ever since they blew away General Obregón, the elected president. But to do that, they didn't make up stories about Outer Mongolia. Toral did it, killed him right there, in front of everybody. Then Toral got whacked. That's something I can understand. What if they'd drummed up all this bullshit about Hong Kong and Outer Mongolia in those days?

"This is very bad for Mexico," the colonel said. "We have transformed the Revolution into a system based on laws, and those laws should not be broken. Do you understand what that means, García? A government subject to the rule of law. That's worth a whole lot more than the lives of a few nutcases."

That guy in the green Fiat parked over there is the same one who's been tailing me. Fucking law! And what's this shit about "We have transformed?" *We* is a lot of people. This jerk was still hanging on his mother's teat when there was real shooting going on. And as far as I can tell, he's still on his mother's teat and he's still trying to figure out whose hide'll yield more whips, or which side of the fan the shit is going to hit. What do these fellows know about making a Revolution, what it was like to be out there dying along those roads?

"A government of laws," the colonel said. "That is what we must preserve at all cost."

Sounds to me like he's practicing his speech for Independence Day. The Revolution hasn't turned into anything. The Revolution is over and now there's nothing but fucking laws. And that's why, no matter where you look, we're all turning into dumbasses. All of us, one way or another. Although with a lot of grace, as the corrido says. As far as I'm concerned, the professor is the only revolutionary left, because he's the only one who doesn't believe in the law. Before, when somebody needed to be whacked, they'd tell it straight, give the order and save the pretty words for their banquets. This fucking colonel is really taking it hard. He's finding out what it's like to give birth on Good Friday, as they say: all by himself he's going to have to find a way. His whole team and his whole laboratory don't do him a bit of good. Now he's fucked. All alone, like a woman in labor. And no matter how hard she pushes, the brat doesn't want to come out.

"Truth is, García, for something like this, I don't have enough men I can trust."

"You've got a lot of men."

"Yeah, but this is special. Call me at ten tonight, I might have some orders for you."

"I wanted to ask for a short leave, Colonel."

"No dice. You've got me thinking about a lot of things, and I have to put some of them in order and check up on others. Call me at ten. I hope you understand that if what you suspect is true, this is one of the most dangerous moments in our history."

"Yes, Colonel."

"I know you have a new girl, a Chinese girl. But that can wait. Be at home at ten and call me."

Fucking colonel! Even he knows about it.

"Where do you want me to drop you off?"

"On Avenida Juárez, Colonel. I'm going home."

"I'll expect your call at ten. Don't fail me and don't leave your house. I might need you sooner."

"Yes, Colonel."

He paid four thousand pesos for the watch, then bought her a gold band, not a very thick one, because Marta has thin wrists.

"Would you like it gift-wrapped?"

"Yes, please, miss."

"Birthday?"

"More like birth."

"Oh, it's for the mother of your grandchild . . ."

The clerk smiled and wrapped the box in white tissue paper, then added a pink bow. I'm going to watch as she opens the box and tries it on. I don't know if I should set it or wait till she's wearing it. That way she'll ask me what time it is. And at ten I'll have to go see the colonel and before that, here on Dolores Street, I'll go see about the dough. And then tomorrow, with what I get, I'll buy Marta a fur coat. Unless by ten the colonel has grown a pair and manages to actually issue an order. Then

Marta will be left alone again, waiting. Fucking colonel! And, what'll I tell Marta? Wait, my dear, I'm just going to go kill a couple of people, I'll be right back. I think I'm going to quit after this. I've got my little stash, and then, if Dolores Street works out … For me and Marta. And then for her alone. I'll have to ask the professor to write me a will. Fucking will! The money for Marta and the memory of all my faithful departed for my grave, right along with me.

He left the shop, walked a block, and turned down Dolores Street. He stopped in front of the address he'd been given. It was Liu's shop—closed, bolted, and barred. He played it shrewd, that fucking Liu. So he's mixed up in that Cuba business. Tonight I'll give him what's coming to him, for Marta and the dough. Damn right they warned me the Chinamen like me because I don't see or hear or talk. Because I'm a dumbass, they should've said.

Santiago was in the restaurant.

"Mr. García, Mr. García!"

García entered and greeted him.

"You look for honorable Mr. Liu?"

"He's not here?"

"No. He no open shop all day and this bad, very bad. You find something about Marta?"

"No."

"I think …"

"Where did Liu go?"

"I no know. I see he go out. Maybe to the Alameda, to the sunshine. You want I go look for him?"

"No, I'll be back later."

He left and took a taxi home. Fucking Liu! Maybe this business with Marta has really gotten to him. But it's weird, because these Chinamen don't care that much about these things. Or maybe he's shaken up about the dough and the killings last night, maybe they were his buddies. Maybe he's already gotten rid of the dough. Fucking Liu! Better to surprise him at night and scare the daylights out of him. If I tell him I'm bringing news of Marta, he'll probably let me in. And he's got no way of knowing that I was involved last night in the killing of his buddies. For sure he'll let me in, even if as a cover-up. And then I'll take the dough. All in fifty-dollar bills.

He arrived home at six in the afternoon. He put the box with the watch in his pocket and walked upstairs to his apartment. He opened the door. The sofa in the living room was covered with boxes and bags from Palacio de Hierro. On the table was a box with three ties in it. García smiled. Damn Marta! I told her to buy things for herself, not for me.

Without making any noise, on tiptoe, he walked over to the door to the bedroom. She must be sleeping. She hasn't gotten used to the hours I keep. She's going to say that I always come when she's sleeping.

The door to the bedroom was ajar.

"Marta!"

Nobody answered. He took the box out of his pocket and pushed the door. She wasn't in the bed. Maybe she's in the bathroom, but there're no sounds from there.

But Marta wasn't in the bathroom. She was on the floor next to the bed, covered in blood, her legs folded up under her, her eyes wide open.

García approached slowly. He kneeled down. He took off his hat and dropped it. Then, with his fingers, he closed her eyes. He picked her up in his arms and put her on the bed. She hadn't been dead long. He stretched out her legs and crossed her arms over her chest. She wasn't bleeding anymore. He took out a clean sheet and covered her with it. A little bit of blood had trickled out of her mouth. He wiped it with his handkerchief. Then he folded the handkerchief neatly and put it back in his pocket. He picked up his hat and placed it on the dresser and placed the box with the watch on the nightstand. Still a little blood was trickling out of her mouth. He wiped it clean again with his handkerchief. He bent over and kissed her on the forehead. Then he covered her face with the sheet and sat down in the chair next to the bed.

His face was set. Like a bitter stone. His hands were crossed on his lap. His eyes began to burn from hatred.

Later, he got up and went into the living room. He gathered together all the things Marta had bought and put them in the closet, where he also put the watch. Then he went back and sat down next to the bed. There was time, lots of time. A while later, he uncovered Marta's face. There was a spot of dried blood on the corner of her lips. He wiped it with his handkerchief, but there was another spot on her cheek. He moistened his handkerchief with some cologne and wiped off the spot. He sat down again.

He pressed his gun against his ribs with his arm. He kept sitting. There was still a lot of time.

At eight-thirty he picked up his hat and left. He carefully closed the door, without making any noise. He went to the garage, where he kept his car. He drove toward Reforma and Colonia Cuauhtémoc. He stopped in a coffee shop where there was a public telephone.

"Mr. del Valle, García here."

"Yes?"

"I've found out something that might interest you ..."

"I thought you were no longer on the case."

"This might interest you."

"What is it?"

"We have to talk face-to-face. It's very important."

"I don't have time. You know that tomorrow—"

"We have to talk, Mr. del Valle. Something's come up, something we hadn't figured on."

"I'm telling you I don't have time."

"Do you want me to tell the Toad and Browning?"

"What?"

"Browning, the gringo you imported. And the Toad, from back home, Mr. del Valle. Or would you prefer I talk to General Miraflores?"

"I don't understand ..."

"I think you sent a message to my house this afternoon, Mr. del Valle. I wasn't there, but when I arrived, I understood the message."

"Do you want money, García?"

"Maybe. But first we need to talk. And I don't want to talk to the gringo or the Toad. I want to talk to you and General Miraflores."

"Okay, fine. Do you know where I live?"

"Yes."

"There's a side door, a door only I use. It's number 64, next to the large gate. Come in half an hour. I'll be waiting for you."

"Good."

"We'll talk here, García."

He hung up the phone. He rushed out and got into the car. Del Valle lived two blocks away. He located the door as he drove by, then parked the car half a block further on and walked back, then waited, hiding in the shadows. Now Marta is alone. She's alone in the bed, alone with her death. I had never thought about that. Killing someone is sending them off to be by themselves, to be alone. They should've killed me, that's what real men do. But they must have thought that one woman is just like any other. And one dead woman is just like the next. That's what they must have thought. But it was Marta. And now she's there alone, with her death. And I was sitting next to her, but she was alone. And I was alone. The two of us. Like a wake! Maybe I should've gotten one of those nuns who sit with the dead. But what would Marta want with a nun now? Fucking nun! Seeing as how you're all alone with your death, you don't need anybody.

A dark Chevrolet stopped in front of number 64 and a military officer got out. García drew his gun and approached as the officer was standing in front of the door.

"Let's go inside, General. I think Mr. del Valle is waiting for us."

"Who are you?"

"Ring the doorbell, General. No reason to talk out here in the street."

At that moment the door opened and del Valle appeared. There was enough light from inside for him to recognize García.

"I told you not to come for half an hour."

"Yes, Mr. del Valle, but here I am. Let's go inside."

They went in and García closed the door. Del Valle said:

"We'll go into my office."

They followed him. The room was large, the walls covered with bookshelves and hung with paintings.

"Have a seat," del Valle said.

He seemed to have recovered his composure.

"I'll stand, if you don't mind, Mr. del Valle," García said.

"Is this García?" the general asked.

"Filiberto García, at your service, General."

"From what they tell me, you've been stirring up trouble. They hired you to conduct an investigation, you did it, and your job is over. If you want some money, a hundred or two hundred pesos, we'll give it to you and that'll be the end of it."

García, still standing, was looking down at General Miraflores. The general felt uncomfortable in his chair. Del Valle sat down behind his desk.

"The whole business was poorly planned, General," García said.

"So, that's what you think. What do you know?"

"The people you hired are no good for a job like this. This time, it's not some two-bit small-town mayor you're trying to get rid of..."

"I don't know what you're talking about, García."

"People like your friends the Toad, Luciano Manrique, and that gringo Browning, General. The Toad and the gringo could expose you. Manrique can't, because I already killed him."

"They don't know anything," del Valle said.

"But they know someone who does know, Mr. del Valle. That's why I'm telling you the whole thing is poorly planned."

"What do you want, García?" the general asked, curtly.

"Are you going to go ahead with your plans?"

"I don't know what you're—"

"It's useless, Miraflores," del Valle interrupted. "García already knows too much."

"Seems you're right."

"Let me think, García."

Del Valle remained sitting behind his desk. Here we are, talking, as if this was just a business deal, and there's Marta all alone.

Alone with her death. For us, time is passing, time is running out, but for Marta, there's no time anymore.

"Look, García," del Valle finally said. "You've said you don't have any political sympathies, that you just follow orders." He was speaking with difficulty, as if he couldn't find the words in his head. "You aren't a Communist and you aren't an anti-Communist, you aren't a friend of the gringos or against the gringos. You just follow orders. The only reason I agreed to let them hire you to work with the Chinese is because they convinced me that was the case. But now I don't understand whose orders you're carrying out. This morning I told you to quit the investigation, and the colonel corroborated. Why have you kept on it?"

"Orders."

"From the colonel?"

"Yes."

"Because of your suspicions?

"Yes."

"I understand. Now, Mr. García, you know that I have more authority than the colonel."

He paused without taking his eyes off García's impassive face or the gun in García's hand.

"I'm going to be the president of the republic, García. It's in your interest to be on friendly terms with the future president, don't you think?"

"Yes, I do."

General Miraflores stood up.

"You are a military man, García, so this will interest you. When Mr. del Valle is president, we military men will return to the position we've always deserved and that the last few civilian governments have taken away from us. And after Mr. del Valle,

I, a military man will be president, because we military men, we soldiers, we are and always have been the most important group in this country. You'd like that, wouldn't you, García?"

"I sure would."

"Then you should help us make that happen," del Valle continued. "When, tomorrow, this minor incident is over, I am going to be president, and we are going to lead Mexico along the road to real progress, with strong and respected authority, and we will have a strong and respectable armed forces."

"An army that will be respected all over the world, García. And you will be part of it," the general asserted.

"As you see," del Valle continued, "we have not become involved in this dangerous mission out of personal interest or ambition. Love of our nation obliges us to act in this way, against our principles. I can assure you that the new government, the one that will take over tomorrow, needs brave men like you—"

"Moreover, García," the general interrupted again, "you should consider this an order, a military order. I speak to you as an army general."

"Yes."

"So, you agree," del Valle affirmed.

"Of course he agrees," the satisfied general said. "One death more, one death less, that's not something that scares off a man like our friend García ..."

The general laughed smugly. García took one step right up to him, and stared at him straight in the eyes.

"There's already been one death too many, General," he said.

The general stopped laughing.

"One death scares you off? I thought you were a man—"

In one quick move of García's hand, the .45 traced a short curve and smashed into the general's face. The gunsight on the

barrel cut into his flesh and blood spurted out. The general stag-
gered backward.

"Don't say that, General. I already told you, there's been one
death too many in this business. Don't put your hand into the
drawer, Mr. del Valle. Come over here, slowly, so you won't be
tempted. And don't you move, General."

"You're crazy, García," del Valle said, approaching him.

"Yes, I am."

"You've always been a hired gun ..."

"Yes, Mr. del Valle. I've always been a hired gun, but now I
told you there was one death too many."

"I thought you were with us, that you agreed to what we were
offering you," del Valle said.

The general wiped the blood off his face. Some had dripped
onto his uniform, possibly staining it for the first time with his
own blood.

"This is going to cost you dearly, García. You don't hit a
Mexican general and get away with it."

García looked at them in silence, his eyes as cold as ice.

"What do you want, García?" del Valle asked. "Everything is
perfectly arranged, and there's just been one minor setback. I
know the police found Browning's hotel."

"Everything is dis-arranged, Mr. del Valle. Better said, everything was dis-arranged from the get-go. Ever since you wanted
to be clever and take advantage of the rumor about the Chinese attack. Ever since you insisted on them hiring me for the
investigation, certain that I would fall right into the trap and
swear there was a Mongolian conspiracy after I woke up from
the blow Luciano Manrique, may he rest in peace, was going
to give me. Ever since you made me work with the gringo and
the Russian. Ever since you chose this general as your partner
and you had him assemble the necessary people, his people,

people who can't even piss straight. And, above all, ever since this afternoon when you sent someone to my house to give me a warning and you killed..."

He paused. Somehow he couldn't pronounce Marta's name in that place.

"Who, García? I swear we didn't send anybody to your house. You were already off the case, you didn't matter anymore."

When García spoke again, his voice was hard as nails.

"You've never killed anybody, Mr. del Valle."

"Of course I haven't."

"Right. That's why you have your hired killers, to kill without thinking, to kill with orders. But for once in your life, I'm going to make you kill."

"Me? You're crazy..."

"They say you should never order anybody else to do something you don't know how to do yourself. And you were going to order someone to assassinate the president..."

"People whose profession it is to kill, García. That's not my profession."

"This is all stupid," the general said.

García hit him in the mouth with his gun.

"Nobody told you to talk, General. Learn to follow orders. What do you say, Mr. del Valle? You want to kill someone to find out how it feels? When you know how it's done, then you'll be able to issue the orders, without making such a fuss."

"I don't understand."

"Your conspiracy has already bit the dust. You and the general together messed up everything. Now not the Chinese or Outer Mongolia or the Russians can be your scapegoats. For that role you need a Mexican, something the people here can understand. Get it now?"

"Yes, but... Everything is in place for the attack."

"Because you already gave the Toad and the gringo their police IDs, so they can be in the square? But that won't work, because the colonel is giving out new ones to the guards."

"Are you sure?"

"Very sure. And if you keep being an important man, who knows, maybe in the next elections you'll make a good showing. Or, who knows, some other time the opportunity will arise and then you'll know how to kill people. Not second-hand, like now."

"What are you proposing, García?"

"That you kill General Miraflores. That you then expose him as the author of the conspiracy. In this way, you will have saved, at the risk of your own life, the life of our president. You will have saved the institutions ... And you'll always have another opportunity."

The general was about to say something, but he looked at García and kept quiet. The blood was pouring down his face and mouth, and his eyes were bloodshot. García kept talking:

"The general is a gunslinger, like me. He's a military man, trained to go around killing people; the only difference, he hides behind his uniform. It's like you said, a killer with a team and the rest of it. But now you can see that doesn't work. He didn't know how to organize anything. You, on the other hand, Mr. del Valle, are a politician who goes around preaching peace and the rule of law. You go around talking about how the Revolution is over and how we are now living in peace ..."

"Yes, that's true ..."

"But, del Valle—" the general started saying.

This time García hit him with the back of his left hand.

"Shut up."

There was silence. The general was having trouble breathing, maybe because of the blood filling his mouth and nose. Maybe because of his sobs.

"If I do what you say—" del Valle said.

"You'll be a hero. Who could beat you in the next elections when everyone will know that at the risk of your own life you saved our institutions? And with time, even you will believe it's all true."

"But ... how?"

"I don't think you'll want to do it with a knife. That's pretty unpleasant. What gun do you have in your drawer?"

"A .32-20."

"A pistol, but it'll work."

García walked over to the desk and pulled out the gun. He walked back, carrying it in his left hand.

"Take it, Mr. del Valle. Shoot him in the chest, three or four times. And don't even think of shooting me. A .45 makes a very big hole."

"I understand," del Valle said.

The general took one step forward.

"Keep still, General."

"Del Valle," he said, "del Valle, we're friends, we've been friends for a long time ..."

Mr. del Valle had the gun in his hand. He was staring at him.

"Del Valle," the general said, "you got me into this mess. The whole idea was yours. I just wanted to help you, as a friend—"

"But you helped me badly, Miraflores," del Valle said. "You did everything badly. In that way, Mr. García's right."

His voice sounded like he was choking, as if it was coming from somewhere far away from his mouth.

"We're friends ..."

"I don't have friends. In politics there are no friendships. And anyway, General Miraflores, after what was going to happen to-morrow, I'd already planned to have you eliminated. It's never a good idea to leave witnesses and I had even thought of hiring Mr. García for the job."

"But I thought—"

"You thought everything wrong, Miraflores. Very wrong."

Mr. del Valle pulled the trigger. The bullet hit the general in his belly. He let out a groan and brought his hands to where he'd been shot. The second bullet didn't hit him. Mr. del Valle had closed his eyes. The general fell slowly to his knees.

"Please, del Valle, for the love of God."

"Now in his chest," García said. "No need to make him suffer."

Mr. del Valle opened his eyes and shot again. The bullet entered the general between his mouth and his nose. The general stretched out his hands and touched del Valle's legs, leaving five red stripes down his pants. Then he fell slowly, headfirst, onto the rug. García walked up and took the gun out of del Valle's hand. Then he took the gun out of the general's holster.

"You see, it's not that difficult, is it?"

Del Valle was staring at the general's body, his eyes spinning.

"Want a drink?"

Del Valle started shaking as if he had severe chills. His teeth were chattering. García when over to a coffee table where there was a small bar service, filled a glass half full of cognac, and brought it to del Valle.

"Here. It's like with women. The first time is tough, but then you start to like it."

Del Valle drank down his cognac in one gulp. He appeared to enjoy it.

"This is terrible."

"When you kill, Mr. del Valle, you are forever condemned to solitude."

"What do you mean?"

"Something I learned this afternoon."

Del Valle didn't take his eyes off the general's dead body.

"Is he dead? I thought I saw him move."

"Want to shoot him again, just to be sure?"

"Give me another cognac."

"Pour it yourself."

Del Valle went over to the table, poured himself a glass, and drank it down in one gulp.

"You don't want one, García?"

"No, I don't need it anymore."

"And now, now what do we do? Maybe the best thing would be to talk to the colonel."

Del Valle's voice was getting stronger, returning to normal:

"Yes, that's it. Thanks to you, Miraflores confessed his villainy to me, his plot to assassinate our president, to overthrow the rule of law. He had his gun in his hand and I had to kill him to defend myself . . . No, to defend our president and our institutions . . ."

Del Valle walked over to the telephone.

"Don't move," García said.

"What do you want now?"

"You, yourself, Mr. del Valle, the first time we talked, you ordered me to get to the bottom of this affair, and if there was truth to the rumors, to act according to my best judgment. I am carrying out your orders."

"But . . . things have changed completely—"

"As for me, one death more or less doesn't matter. The only death that does matter happened this afternoon, Mr. del Valle . . ."

"I told you, I didn't give those orders, I didn't know any-thing—"

"Maybe. But we can't be left with any doubts. I can't. And then, you just killed General Miraflores."

"You forced me to, García."

"General Miraflores came with me, Mr. del Valle, to arrest you for conspiring against the life of our president, and you killed him in cold blood. I killed you, trying to save General Miraflores."

"You can't kill me, García."

"I can't?"

"You just made me kill a man ..."

"Yes, I did. It was good for you to know what it felt like and for me to know what I can expect from you."

"I can give you whatever you want, García. You yourself say I'll have other opportunities to become president. I can make you rich when I'm president—"

"President of hell, Mr. del Valle."

He fired one shot. The bullet entered del Valle right between the eyes, smashed his face, and shattered, along with his eyeglasses, the appearance of a venerable and important man. García placed the gun in the dead hand of the general and put away his own. Then he went to the telephone on the desk and dialed a number:

"Colonel, García here."

"It's seven minutes after ten, García. I told you to call me at ten on the dot."

"Any orders, Colonel?"

"We haven't been able to arrest the Toad or the gringo, but I'm certain you were right. We picked up the rifle—"

"Any orders, Colonel?"

"Yes. We have to arrest them, arrest them any way we can. I've changed all the guards, just in case. I've asked the FBI to send reinforcements to station guards in the windows overlooking the square. But we have to arrest the leaders ..."

"That will no longer be necessary, Colonel."

"What do you mean? This is an order..."

"I'm at del Valle's house. Seems there was a disagreement, words were spoken, and they shot each other."

"Are they dead?"

"Yes."

"Wait for me there."

"I'm sorry, Colonel, but there's a couple of things I have to do."

He hung up the phone, left the room, and reached the door to the street. He had put his gun back in its holster. When he opened the door, he found himself face-to-face with two men. Both had their guns drawn.

"Don't move," one of them said. "Inside..."

García stepped back, without taking his eyes off them. The two men entered behind him.

"We heard some shots. Where are Mr. del Valle and General Miraflores?"

"There, inside," García said.

"You're García," one of the men said. "I've seen around."

"Yeah, and you're the Toad..."

"*So, this is the guy,*" the other said in English.

"And this gentleman is Mr. Browning."

"Let's go to the office," said the Toad.

They went to the office. The gringo let out a quick whistle when he saw the corpses.

"You did them both in," the Toad said.

"They killed each other," García said.

The gringo, without letting go of his gun, approached the general and took his .45 out of its holster.

"*He hasn't fired,*" he said in English, smelling the butt.

"I received your message," García said. "When I arrived

home this afternoon, I received your message."

"We haven't sent you any message, García. But right now we're going to send you straight to hell."

"You didn't go to my house this afternoon?"

"We don't even know where you live. We've been running around all day. They descended on us at the hotel—"

"*Shut up,*" the gringo said. You, *Mister García*, you are going to die today ..."

"If we'd known where your house was, we'd have gone there to kill you," the Toad said. "Anyway, I've been wanting to do this for a while, ever since you killed Luciano Manrique."

"How did you know it was me?"

"Mr. del Valle told me. And now, sit still, this won't hurt, just like the doctors say—"

At the open door, Laski's voice rang out.

"Need some help, Filiberto?"

The gringo turned quickly and Laski's bullet hit him right in the heart, throwing him backward. The Toad jumped on García, but he already had his knife out and the Toad fell on it, pushing it into his chest. García pulled it out and stabbed him again. Laski grabbed his arm.

"Let's go, Filiberto."

García picked up his gun, and they ran out. They could hear the police sirens a ways away.

"Let's take your car," Laski said.

They got in. At that very moment, two police patrols arrived at Mr. del Valle's house. García started the engine.

"Thanks," García said.

"Are you hurt?" Laski asked.

"No."

"I understand that this business was between Mexicans, Filiberto, but I found myself obliged to intervene. You are my friend."

"I thought you weren't sentimental."

Laski chuckled.

"I need you. For what I told you at noon. And when I need something, I take care of it, like my Luger."

"Thanks, anyway."

"I've managed to find out who the phone number 3-5-9-9-0-8 belongs to," Laski said.

García looked at him, surprised.

"Yes, Filiberto. It's the number that Chinese man dialed, when he asked for the money he was going to bribe us with. The phone belongs to another Chinese man, someone named Liu, who lives on Dolores Street."

"Yeah."

"And Miss Fong worked for that man, before going to you."

"So what?"

"I want you to help me with this investigation. They've told me you are a friend of Liu's."

"I'm done with my investigation."

"No, no, you aren't."

"Yes, yes, I am."

"Miss Fong is dead, Filiberto."

There was silence. Yes. Marta is dead, and alone with her death. There in my bed. And me here alone with my life. And del Valle and the general and all the others are also alone with their deaths. And me, alone with my life. It's like they're leaving me behind. It's like I'm always standing at the door, opening it for others who are already alone with their deaths. But I stay outside, always outside. And now Marta already went inside and I'm still outside.

"Look, Filiberto, I think Liu sent Miss Fong to watch you, to keep an eye on your activities, thinking that you were investigating this business with Cuba ..."

"Who killed her?"

"A Chinese man entered your house around five this afternoon. Shall we go find Liu?"

"Yes."

They reached Dolores Street. The shops and restaurants were closed and nobody was outside. *They probably took my advice and everyone's hiding. It's like everyone decided to leave us alone. And Marta alone with her death and me alone with my life.*

They stopped in front of Liu's shop and got out of the car. They knocked on the door. A few moments later it opened. It was Liu. He looked at García and then at the Russian, his face expressionless. The shop was almost dark, lit only by a Chinese brazier filled with charcoal and burning papers. It smelled of smoke and incense. Liu stepped back to let them enter, then closed the door and turned to his visitors.

"Marta is dead," García said.

"Yes."

"You killed her?"

"Yes."

García slowly drew his gun. Laski intervened.

"What papers are you burning?"

"Paper, bad paper, very bad paper ..."

They walked up to the brazier. A large stack of fifty-dollar bills was burning on the coals. There were still two or three tea tins full of bills, and several others already empty.

"Very bad paper," Liu said.

García raised his gun. Laski intervened.

"Just a moment, Filiberto ..."

"Let him, sir. Better like this ..."

"Why did you send that girl to watch over García?"

"What it matter?"

He threw another fistful of bills on the coals, the room lit up, and the white porcelain bellies of the Buddhas lined up in the window were glowing.

"Are you working with Wang and that gang?"

"What it matter?"

"What did you want to know about García?"

"My son dead ... what matter else? My oldest son ... And you killed him ... My son Xavier ..."

"Your son, Liu? I didn't know you had a son," García said.

Liu threw more bills on the flames.

"He lived in Cuba ... And Marta ran away and she give him to you. And now he dead ... He my only son and now finished honorable house of Liu. Now nobody to continue to pray for honorable ancestors. That what happen when you kill my son, Xavier. And Marta like every woman, bad, very bad. She fall in love with you, Mr. García, but this no matter now. Everyone know woman is bad from birth, very bad, traitor. But then she give you my son, Xavier, who come from Cuba full of dream to do important thing there, very important. And he give me this bad money to keep ..."

He threw some more bills on the fire, then leaned over to blow on the flames. Laski grabbed his jacket and forced him to stand up.

"Who was the leader of this business with Cuba?"

"What matter now? You kill my son, Xavier ... What matter the other?"

"Who was the leader?" Laski insisted.

"What matter ...?"

Laski smashed him across the face with the butt of his gun, but Liu didn't seem to notice. He didn't even bring his hands to his face. García stepped forward and forced Laski to let Liu go.

"Why did you kill Marta?"

"She bad, very bad. She sold my son, Xavier ..."

"She didn't tell me anything about your son."

Liu stood in silence, as if pondering his words. The blood was running down onto his chest. He leaned over and threw more bills on the fire.

"She tell me she going to stay with you, because you good ... I don't believe her. Women always tell lie ... She told you about Xavier and he dead ..."

García fired. The Chinaman fell against the window, broke the glass, and the porcelain Buddhas fell to the ground. García put his gun in the holster and left the shop. Some lights went on and a few Chinese cautiously peeked out their windows. A police siren could be heard from far away. García left the car where it was and walked toward Avenida Juárez. His hands were hanging by his sides, heavy, like two useless items. I have to wash my hands. Why keep carrying around other people's blood? It's not right to go to her with my hands covered with blood. She might get frightened. Fucking hands!

Laski caught up with him at the corner of Avenida Juárez.

"You shouldn't have done that, Filiberto."

García kept walking. He turned right, toward Cinco de Mayo and La Ópera cantina. Laski walked alongside him.

"You shouldn't have done that. It was important to find out everything possible about this Chinese conspiracy."

García kept walking. My hands are heavy, too heavy, as if I were carrying stones. Liu killed her. I killed Liu. My hands are heavy. They hurt, too many deaths all together. I feel like sitting down on this bench ... on a rock in the open fields, like before, by the side of the road. But there are no more roads to walk down with my heavy hands, my aching hands from all the dead I carry around with me. Fucking hands!

"That wasn't professional what you did today, Filiberto. You must get everything you possibly can out of a suspect before killing him. That's elementary."

García crossed San Juan de Letrán. In Yurécuaro I would sit on a rock next to the train tracks. My hands weren't heavy then. I could throw stones against the rails. I could climb the orange trees and pick stolen fruit. My fucking hands weren't so heavy.

"Or maybe your government gave you orders not to get to the bottom of it. Or maybe the Americans … It would be sad if you, a Mexican, were working for the gringos. They are your real enemies."

García turned down Condesa Alley. And here I am with my hands so heavy, walking down the street. And she in my bed, alone with her death. And me alone, walking down the street, my hands as heavy as the many dead. And nothing's heavy for her anymore, not time, not nothing. Or maybe her death is heavy, as if a man were on top of her. I don't know what that's like, death. She does now. That's why she's alone. That's why she's not with me. Because she knows and I don't. All I know is how to start down this road, how to live carrying my solitude. Fucking solitude!

Laski grabbed his arm:

"You have to listen to me, García."

García stopped and turned around. His hat shadowed his face.

"Look, if your government ordered you to act this way, I have nothing to say, I understand you. But otherwise, if it's for personal reasons, sentimental reasons … For Miss Fong … That's just not professional! None of us kills for reasons like that. It would be absurd. It would be criminal."

García said:

"Go fuck yourself and your mother!"

Then he turned and started walking again. Laski stood there, watching him go.

At La Ópera cantina, the professor said to him:

"The colonel is looking for you, Cap'n."

The professor was very drunk. His voice was slurred and his eyes unfocused.

"Give me a bottle of cognac," García asked the man at the bar.

Only a few clients were there. The cantina was getting ready to close.

"You've got blood stains on your clothes, Cap'n," the professor said.

García opened the bottle of cognac and poured himself a glass.

"In the old days, lawyers always had ink stains on their hands and their clothes. Occupational hazard. But we don't use ink anymore. We use typewriters. You people should find some equivalent system. Our whole civilization tends toward allowing us to keep our hands clean ... At least, our hands."

García gulped down a shot of cognac and closed the bottle. Fucking professor! He's never been afraid of me or, maybe, he's looking for a way to die. Maybe he's the only one who's really got any balls, at least when he's drunk. But Marta is alone in my bed. Alone with her death.

"Come with me, Professor. We're going to a wake."

"Did you supply the deceased?"

"Come on."

He picked up the bottle of cognac, paid, and they walked out.

When they entered the house, García didn't turn on the light. Enough was coming in through the window. He went into the kitchen and washed his hands. Shouldn't go to her with this blood on my hands. With all this fucking blood.

The professor was dozing off in the living room.

"Where's the deceased, Cap'n?"

"Come with me."

They went into the bedroom. The light from the window shone on the bed and the inscrutable shape of the corpse under the sheet. García pulled two chairs up to the foot of the bed. He told the professor to sit down in one of them. Then he went into the kitchen and brought two glasses, filled them with cognac, and gave one to the professor. He sat down, holding the other one.

"Thank you," the professor said.

"Say a prayer, Professor."

"What prayer? I can't remember any..."

"I'm asking you as my friend. Just pray, even if there aren't any candles."

The professor began to recite something, like he used to when he was an altar boy. The words came out all mixed up, slurred from the booze.

"*Requiem eternam dona eis Domine.*"

García took a long slug. The gun pressed against his heart. Fucking wake! Fucking solitude!

A note about the author

While working on this translation, Katherine Silver, with the kind help of Francisco Prieto, got in touch with the author's offspring. Bernal's youngest daughter, Cocol, offered insights into her father's idiosyncratic use of certain terms and turns of phrase and also generously shared some family lore. New Directions asked if her stories could be added as an afterword to The Mongolian Conspiracy. *Cocol agreed, "with the caveat that I am speaking from the myopic perspective of a fifteen-year-old, tinged by family history, interpretation of memories, and some stories my Aunt Lola (a very creative woman), my dad (also very creative), and my Uncle Luis (a lawyer—not so creative) told me. I am conscious that my reality is very much my own, from a very narrow vantage point. Just some loose insights that anyone is welcome to. Or as the Italians say: Si non e vero e ben trovato. (If it's not true, it's a good find.)" Asked about her father's political affiliations, his philias or phobias, as del Valle asked Feliberto, Cocol replied, "It's a complicated story."*

215

My family, on my father's mother's side, were ultra-right-wing monarchists and devout Catholics. In the mid-1800's, my great-great grandfather, the historian Don Joaquín García Icazbalceta, who owned seven sugar haciendas in Morelos (of which Santa Ana de Tenango still remains in the family), made a bet with a cousin that he could turn a healthy profit while treating his workers decently—even giving them above-average wages, their own land, medical care, and no company store. The experiment was a success and he made a profit. He didn't convince anyone else to try it as he had hoped, but as a result the family is still very respected in the village of Tenango. He saw this as his social and Christian duty. He later came afoul of the Church when the bishop ordered him to write a historical account of the Virgin of Guadalupe. He complied but told the bishop that faith and history do not mix and although in his heart he believed in the Virgin, the historian in him could not justify her existence other than as a myth. He wrote that there was absolutely no historical proof of the apparition. I believe he was excommunicated, and I do know that most of his friends deserted him.

Partly as a result of this and to regain acceptance into Mexican society, my great grandfather, Don Luis García Pimentel, became an almost fanatical right-wing Catholic. His daughter, my grandmother, Doña Rafaela Garcia Pimentel y Elguero, even gave our best hacienda (Santa Clara de Montefalco) to the Opus Dei. Anyway, Don Joaquín's experiment has been a source of great pride in the family.

The Bernals were very very rich landowners from Tlaxcala who came to save the decaying García Pimentel family from penury: although they went along with it, the Bernals did not particularly share the García Pimentels' enthusiasm for Catholicism—my grandfather, Rafael Bernal y Bernal, being a bon vivant of great proportions.

Then, in the third year of my grandparents' Paris honeymoon, the revolution started and their world was completely turned upside down. The García Pimentels lost most of their lands and, later, so did the Bernals. There was hunger followed by the disillusionment of the post-revolution period.

My father grew up with a devout mother and a hedonistic father who adored each other and traveled constantly. My father became a mix of both: an intellectual who devoured Nietzsche and Sartre, spoke Latin fluently, and was a devout Catholic, too. He was big in the Sinarquista movement of the '40s and '50s—he was actually very proud of having been in jail eighteen times for "disolución social." He was fiercely opposed to Benito Juárez, believing that the separation of church and state robbed the nation of its soul. He was also a supporter of Franco. So you can say he was very right wing. At the same time, with my uncle Ignacio Bernal (a famous archaeologist), he made a lot of money out of cheating foreigners at bridge and paraded a series of very elegant and expensive mistresses.

Not sure what exactly happened in the '50s, but he left Sinarquismo and wrote a poem repudiating his support of Franco. He went to trial for defacing the statue of Juárez on the Alameda (he hired mountain climbers to drape a hood and a noose over Juárez) and was pardoned by Miguel Alemán (a pardon which he refused on the basis that he hadn't done anything illegal). Then, in 1956, he met my mother, who was a young divorcee working in radio, and that was it. He left the Church (and his current mistress, the Princess Agatha of Ratibor) in order to marry her.

I was born in 1957 in Caracas to an atheist father, who was by then left-leaning, and an agnostic mother, both of whom proudly had me baptized in the cathedral in the very font where Simón Bolívar had been baptized. So . . . go figure.

He remained a searching man, struggling between his beliefs, family loyalties, his own deep intellectual curiosities, and an openness to new ideas, which did not, however, extend to accepting my brother's pink shirts.

He really believed in women's rights. I never heard him say that I couldn't do something because I was a girl. On the contrary, he pushed me to read and write, and I just had to mention a book, and the next day it would be mine. Any intellectual pursuit was encouraged. He expected from me the same as from my brothers.

I asked him once whether he was left or right. He said that what had once been left was now right. At fourteen I was not going to say that I had no idea what he meant, so I inquired no further.

I think that being a diplomat freed him from having to declare political affiliations. He represented the government and he did that well. Within these parameters, he did manage to express himself quite freely intellectually. He was a man who, given a good reason, was not afraid to change his mind and he did so often.

Then, at the end of his life, in 1971, he did go back to the Church. I didn't understand it at the time, but now I think he was reaching for comfort before death.

Around the time my father was writing *El complot mongol,* we lived in Lima. The military coup that toppled Belaunde's first administration had just happened and the military junta was in power. My dad hated the military (any military) with passion. He thought they were subhuman.

My dad wrote *El complot mongol* in about a month, taking a break from writing a history of the Pacific Ocean, *El gran oceano,* which he had been working on for over twenty years. (*El gran oceano* was published by El Fondo de Cultura Económica: it's about the cultural exchanges along the Pacific throughout the centuries.)

When *El complot mongol* came out in 1968, my dad was First Secretary at the Mexican Embassy in Lima. A lot of junior bureaucrats at the Ministry of Foreign Affairs in Mexico City had read the book and were calling for my father's head on a platter, because they were convinced that del Valle was meant to be Minister Carrillo Flores. My dad, summoned to Mexico, gave Carrillo Flores a copy of the book. Carrillo Flores loved the book and gave it to all his friends for Christmas. Dad summed it up with one of his sayings—*Al que le quede el saco, que se lo ponga.* (More or less: If the shoe fits, wear it.)

And while we are at it, the tale about killing someone and then trying to sneak the dead body out of town in a coffin only to have the corpse awaken is a real story. My dad spent lots of time in the jungles of Quintana Roo and Chiapas and met many guns for hire who, after a few tequilas, were more than happy to tell him all their stories. A lot of Filiberto's stories come from them.

One last anecdote: The official-for-home-use-only name of the book is *"El pinche complot mongol."* We all call it that, including Dad, who was very proud of the ending *"¡Pinche velorio! ¡Pinche soledad!"*

COCOL BERNAL